SHE CAN'T TELL

CARLA WHEIN

Publishing Services provided by Paper Raven Books
Printed in the United States of America
First Printing, 2020

Paperback ISBN: 978-1-7354465-0-9
Hardback ISBN: 978-1-7354465-1-6

CHAPTER 1

"Alexis, truth or dare?"

"Kendra, we're forty-three, not twelve." I topped off our glasses with the remains of our third bottle of wine. I slid my barstool closer to the kitchen island to keep my eyes out of the direct path of the setting autumn sun. With Kendra's head now blocking the sun, I saw a playful and mischievous look in her eyes.

"Come on Lex, it'll be fun," Kendra said with wide eyes and raised eyebrows.

"Kendra, we're not kids anymore. Plus, I'm an Air Force officer with a standard to enforce."

Kendra slithered around the granite-topped island and leaned into me. With knowing eyes she slurred, "Doll, you and I both know damn well how strictly you've complied with that military standard, so truth or dare?"

Her sarcasm was not lost on me, but this scene was a little too familiar. My best friend, Kendra, spending the night and pushing the boundaries of our friendship. Playing truth or dare at forty-something years old was one thing. Playing the game that had launched my own sexual discovery was another. Kendra and I had survived a tumultuous few decades as friends. Yet, here we were, together again, this time on the eve of my retirement from a twenty-year career in the Air Force, still friends despite the hell she had put me through.

Not that the next career was going to be much different. Same job, different uniform. I'd be going back to the Pentagon wearing an urban assault uniform, also known as "civilian clothes."

I wasn't thrilled about the adventurous move to doing the same damn job in the same damn place with the same damn people. But the skills were familiar, the relationships were built, and I'd still have the title of Air Force Lieutenant Colonel, just with "retired" at the end.

The "retired" suffix provided protection from a title of "inmate" and that had to count for something. At least I couldn't be punished for who I was. Any disciplinary action I received as a civilian contractor would be due to a legitimate crime like embezzlement, money laundering, or racketeering.

I hated to leave the uniformed service, but two decades of paranoia had taken their toll. I loved my military teammates, our global mission, and the experiences and opportunities, but hated the compromises I felt I had to make to survive.

- 3 -

CHAPTER 2

The last time we had played truth or dare was a couple weeks after our graduation from high school. It was me, Kendra, and our third musketeer, Franny. Kendra usually dictated the plans for our evenings, and twenty-four years earlier, truth or dare was on the agenda, and my response hadn't been much different.

"Kendra, we're seventeen, not twelve." I tucked my sleeping bag under my legs in preparation for what would be another long round of this silly game.

"Come on Lex, it'll be fun. Just like old times." Franny had always been a fan of the slumber party and the monosyllabic nickname.

"Three intelligent women playing a sixth grader's game. To think we're the top three graduates of Bishop Westmoreland High School's class of '87 just days away from starting college," I said.

"Ha. It's only days for you, Lex. We've got the whole summer off. Only you'd pick a school that started at the beginning of summer." Kendra had a knack for ribbing me about choices I made, even though she was proud of my decisions. Calling the end of June the "beginning of summer" was also very Kendra-esque. But then again "morning" for her was most people's one p.m. Her timelines were just a tad different from the rest of society's. As were her standards for herself. Despite graduating third in our class, she was headed for the ever-rigorous community college three miles from home, where she would be challenging herself with eight credit hours.

Franny, our valedictorian, was bound for a nearby college, with her sights set on becoming a fashion designer.

Kendra was more than content to have no significant academic aspirations or goals for her grown-up life. However, she was my number-one cheerleader and my number-one critic, the dual role solely reserved for her.

Kendra's straightforward approach to life and our friendship were evident from the day we met when she pulled out my loose baby tooth. We were in first grade at recess, and friends were gathered around to see my tooth dangling by a fiber of flesh. Kendra was a friend of a friend, and intrigued by the spectacle, moved herself to the front of the pack. She had reached her hand up to my bared smile, pulled the tooth, and offered it to me in a handshake as she introduced herself, "Hey, I'm Kendra, your new best friend."

The addition of Franny during the fifth grade had been Kendra's choice too. Franny's Barbie-doll good looks didn't match her above-average intelligence. Even though she tried to overcompensate her book smarts with a ditzy level of street smarts, other kids in the school had made fun of her.

Kendra reached out to Franny in the same matter-of-fact way she had reached out to me, and with one, "Blondie, get over here and sit with us" in the lunchroom, Franny completed our threesome.

Franny was usually the butt of Kendra's jokes and the victim of Kendra's pranks, but like the addict of an abusive relationship, Franny remained Kendra's faithful follower. She usually kept her head in the clouds, somehow unable to process decisions made by others that she would never make for herself.

"What were you thinking, girl? Ain't you nervous about going to the Air Force Academy? Wearing combat boots all summer and playing war. Who does that?" Franny asked.

"Of course she's nervous," Kendra started. "The academy isn't easy to get in to, and our little Lexy did it. She's gonna kick ass and make us proud, aren't ya, doll?" Kendra pushed my hair back behind my ear while she answered for me as she usually did.

"So are we gonna play?" Franny got us back on track. "Lex, truth or dare?"

"Fine. Truth." Franny's questions usually lacked creativity, so there was no harm in challenging her to come up with something.

"Are you nervous about going to the academy next week?" Franny asked. Case in point.

Kendra interrupted. "What a fucking waste of a question, Franny. I just told you she was nervous. Ask another question."

"Oh. Um, do you like my new haircut?" Franny tried again.

"Holy fucking shit, Franny. You never did understand this game. You just lost your turn. Lex, I dare you to kiss me," Kendra said.

"Ken, I said 'truth' not 'dare,' and you are not getting that dick licker anywhere near me."

Franny giggled and watched while twirling locks of her long blonde hair.

Kendra fit, or probably created, the loose Catholic schoolgirl stereotype. Our senior year started off with her popping into first-period physics class late after a first date with a guy she had just met.

"How was your date last night?"

"Ask me where I woke up?" she winked.

And here, two semesters later, before I knew it, Kendra had positioned herself in front of me, and her lips were on mine. Her tongue popped inside my mouth and sent goose bumps to every part of my body.

I had never once considered that any women had been part of her reputation building.

Until now.

Unable to think about anything other than her soft, experienced lips on mine, I shut my eyes and neither returned nor fought the kiss.

Kendra gently squeezed my shoulders, and just as I leaned into her kiss, she pulled away abruptly.

When I opened my eyes, I was breathless, speechless, turned on, and confused.

"Not bad," Kendra said.

And then I was pissed.

I wiped the kiss off my lips with disgust. "I'm done playing this stupid game. I'm going to sleep."

"Lex, why are you blushing?" Franny asked.

"I'm not blushing." Which I knew was a lie. I could feel the heat in my face and all over my body.

"What's the big deal?" Franny persisted, "We always play this game, and I had to kiss Kendra once too."

"Franny, don't flatter yourself. You pecked me with puckered-up lips and squinty eyes." Kendra's words confirmed my thought that the kiss she and I had just shared wasn't the same kind of kiss she and

Franny had shared. "If Lex wants to stop playing and go to sleep, we'll let her. At least she'll have sweet dreams."

"Good. I'm tired, too, but you guys have to promise not to make me pee in my sleep again." Franny's whine was a reminder of every slumber party where Kendra threatened to put the hand of the first sleeper in warm water. Franny was usually the first to fall asleep and therefore the normal mark of Kendra and her bowl of water. Even on the nights where I was the first one down, Kendra would wait until Franny fell asleep, then wake me up to watch her put Franny's hand in the bowl in the hopes of making her wet her sleeping bag.

Kendra rolled her eyes, laughed, then tucked Franny into her sleeping bag. "Night, Franny."

"Night, Ken. Night, Lex." Franny was snoring within minutes.

The glow from the clock of the VCR lit Kendra's way as she navigated her way to her sleeping bag lying next to mine.

"Why'd you do that, Ken?" I whispered as Kendra settled in next to me.

"What?" Kendra innocently asked.

"You know what."

"What's the big deal? You didn't seem like you minded it."

"Well, I did."

"Lexy, I just wanted to show you who you were before you went off to that academy."

"And who is it that I am?"

"You're a dyke, and you won't admit it."

I hated that word. It conjured up images of she-men with crew cuts, girls born female but deeply desiring to be men. I hated it more because it was coming from Kendra, my supposed best friend, who used the vile word to describe me. I rolled onto my side, with my back toward her. She shimmied closer and pinned my shoulder down, forcing me to my back and forcing me to look into her face.

"Lexy, it's okay. I know you're into chicks. I've known since we were fourteen. I love you anyway. I just want you to be comfortable with it."

"Kendra, shut up and go to sleep." I tried to push her away, but remnant thoughts of our very recent kiss weakened me.

"Fine. Goodnight." Kendra pushed my bangs away from my face as she brought her face closer. She teased me with a brief, soft kiss and then planted a firmer, longer kiss on my lips. This time I returned the kiss with seventeen years' worth of passion to do what I was doing right then: kissing another woman.

My hands ran feverishly through Kendra's hair. Our moans went unnoticed by Franny, still snoring a few feet away. I rolled on top of Kendra, took both her hands, and held them above her head. The forcefulness seemed to startle Kendra in a good way, as I heard her gasp, "Damn, Lex."

Holding Kendra's hands together and out of the way with my left hand, I guided Kendra's chin back to my mouth to continue our kiss. Our tongues flicked in and out of each other's mouths as my body writhed against hers. Kendra had always prided herself as the best kisser of the group, and we had just taken her word for it, but now I had firsthand knowledge of this very true fact. My kissing total up to this point in my life was four, but none of those kisses came as naturally nor were as passionate as this. Oh, and none of those kisses had been with another girl, and what better way to explore such a thing than with your best friend.

My right hand shocked me as it boldly moved down to caress Kendra's large chest.

"Oh God, Lex," Kendra cried out. She broke an arm out of what I thought was a firm grip, and her free hand pushed my head down to her tits. I eagerly pushed Kendra's shirt up, and my hand tended to Kendra's left tit while my mouth consumed the other.

This wasn't the first time I had seen Kendra's bare chest. Years of being on the same sports teams had brought up countless opportunities of changing clothes together. We had wiggled into basketball uniforms in the back of her parents' station wagon and huddled together under a blanket while changing into soccer jerseys before games. The sight of Kendra's tits had always inspired some unidentifiable feeling inside me, but I diagnosed it as jealousy, thinking I just wanted bigger boobs like hers. Now I realized that I did want boobs like hers, not on my chest as my own, but in my mouth and hands as they were right now.

I traced warm wet circles around Kendra's nipple with my tongue while she held my head in approval. The sounds that came from Kendra's throat only fueled me further. Her moan was unmistakably caused by pleasure and encouraged me to suck and twist her tits harder. I was lost in the moment.

Lost, until I heard Kendra's sultry voice. "Doll, I knew you were a dyke."

That word. That disgusting word. Of all the possible suggestions a thesaurus could generate, it was my very least preferred. I became very conscious of the moment, and all at once, my mouth and hand stopped. My whole body became rigid as I shifted my body to glare into Kendra's eyes.

"Come on, doll. Don't stop, you're doing great." Kendra's desperate whisper sounded like a hiss as she tried to push my head back to her chest.

"I think our experiment just ended, Ken. Good night."

I rolled off of Kendra and into my sleeping bag. My heart pounded, and my crotch throbbed with unattained passion. The illuminated clock revealed that it had been nearly twenty minutes since Kendra had crawled over to me. I spent the next restless hours trying to remember the last time Kendra had pissed me off so badly. I had a rich assortment of case studies since Kendra was always pissing me off one way or another. We would go days without talking until Kendra made the first move to repair what she had broken.

But this time was different. It didn't feel like a petty thing that normally put us into friendship breakups. This was a more significant event.

She had unearthed something I had buried long ago. Feelings I wasn't allowed to have according to the God my church worshipped. Feelings I wasn't allowed to have according to the school I was about to begin. Feelings I wasn't allowed to have according to the employer who would hopefully get twenty years of my life after school.

The morning arrived after a sleepless night, and I was determined that this breakup would last longer than normal. Except for some tense small talk as Kendra and Fanny left, I refused to acknowledge

Kendra's presence. I wanted her to know how far over the line she had crossed by kissing me and calling me a dyke.

CHAPTER 3

"Alexis, what's troubling you honey?" Mom asked.

"She's just nervous about heading off to school," Dad cut in.

"Why would she be nervous, Gene? She's going to do great."

"Of course she's going to do great. Are you telling me that she's not going to be nervous going to the Air Force Academy?"

"Oh, I'm sure she's going to be nervous, I didn't say she wouldn't be. I just wondered if something was troubling her right now," Mom said.

"She's just nervous, and too smart to be concerned with anything else but focusing on the academy. Alexis, tell your mother I'm right."

"Dad's right, Mom."

"Oh, okay. I just love you honey, and I'm so proud of you." Mom was interrupted by the loud, distinctive chortle of Kendra's Mustang. "Who's here? We're not expecting company, are we? See who that is, honey."

"Sounds like Kendra's car, Darlene."

"You didn't even look up." Mom strained to straighten her back enough to see over the hedges.

Dad shook his head as he rolled his eyes. "Kendra's been driving that loud Rust-Oleum–colored Mustang since the girls got their licenses, Darlene. Who else has a car that sounds like a herd of wounded wildebeest?"

"Oh." Mom straightened her long skirt out as she stood to greet Kendra at the door, failing to sense my discomfort with Kendra's arrival.

"How are you, dear?" Mom bear-hugged Kendra as she did every time Kendra came over.

"Fine, Mrs. Erecat. Is Lexy home?"

"You girls go on up to her room. Mr. Erecat and I don't want to eavesdrop on which boy you're sweet on this week." Mom winked and giggled.

I shot Dad a look pleading for rescue. From Mom. From Kendra.

He narrowed his eyes and cocked his head like he had thousands of times before when I wanted to quit a task, a sport, a class, or anything challenging. The early days of "the look" had been accompanied by a paternal lecture about finishing what we start, about facing the harder right and not escaping with a cowardly evasion.

I hated when he was right. He was making me a better person and would help make me a better leader. That was on him.

"Come on Lexy," Kendra led the way up the stairs.

I followed her because, although I was still appalled by her stunt two nights earlier, I was also curious about her presence and desperate to keep my parents, well at least my mom, from knowing anything had happened.

Life in Mom and Dad's black-and-white conservative Mayberry would be completely disheveled if they learned their child had engaged in the heinous act of a same-sex kiss. Their world would cease to revolve if they knew that kiss had been lying in want for a lifetime.

Kendra plopped herself onto my bed the way she had done thousands of times before, only this time was different, and only I seemed to realize that.

"Whaddaya, want Ken?"

"Don't be pissed off about the other night, Lexy. I just want you to be comfortable with who you are before you head off to that right-wing, Republican, dyke-hating school you chose to go to."

"Ken, don't. I don't wanna talk about it, and I sure as hell don't wanna hear about it from you."

"Look, Lexy, I know that for some reason, you feel all this pressure to be a superwoman prove-it-all, and you live your life for your parents' approval. God forbid their only child deviate from the Catholic norm, but this is who you are, Lex, and we both know it."

"Ken, stop." I tried to cut her off.

Kendra's voice got sincere. "Lex, you've exceled at everything you've touched. Shit knows you've beaten me at anything we've competed over. You're my very best friend, and I love you and will love you til the end. But part of my love is honesty and showing you who you are."

"Why the hell would you wait until the last minute like this? I busted my ass to get in to the academy, Ken. I'm not gonna jeopardize my chance at an Air Force career by having you fill my head with this bullshit idea that I'm into chicks and not guys! Is this your last-ditch attempt to get me to stay in this dead-end town with you so we can both amount to nothing and work at a fucking drive-through window for the rest of our lives?"

"Lexy, come on. I want the best for you and I want you to be happy, but if you go through this academy and through the rest of your life pretending you're straight, you'll never be happy. Think about it, Lex. Think back on the boys you've dated, think back on the feelings you've had for them, think back on the feelings you've had for me. I know you, Lex. I know you better than you know yourself."

She was right about that. She did know me better than anyone else and admittedly, probably knew me better than I knew myself. I refused to let her be right about this. Not after all the work I'd done to get into my first-choice school.

"Is this about you being in love with me and wanting me to be yours or something sick and twisted like that?" I took a stab in the dark. Not that it couldn't work out between us. We had been inseparable since the first-grade tooth-pulling introduction. I remember feeling no pain from the loss of the tooth, confusion from the odd introduction, and excitement that someone wanted to be my best friend. But it had started the roller coaster of friendship with Kendra. Her brazenness complemented my law-abiding nature. She was the first person I wanted to celebrate victories with and seek comfort in. No one could make me laugh like Kendra could, and no one could piss me off like Kendra could.

"You wish, babe." Kendra laughed. "I just want you to be happy. You'll never be happy until you figure out who you are, and I'm just helping you on that path."

"Well, Ken, you're wrong. Don't talk about what it is you think I am or what it is you think makes me happy. For a best friend, you don't know shit about me." I hoped that my trembling voice didn't betray the lies I was spewing.

"Calm down, doll." The sound of that moniker evoked a flood of pre-puke spit into my mouth. My stomach rumbled with threats of rejecting my last meal.

"Don't call me that."

"I've called you that for as long as I can remember." Kendra reached out a hand and lightly stroked my arm.

"Well remember to stop calling me that, and don't ever touch me again."

"Jesus, Lex. Someday you're going to realize how fucking dead on tits I am about you, and you're gonna have to come crawling back with a shitload of apologies."

"Well until then, Kendra, get the hell out of my house, and don't hold your breath waiting for me to come crawling back."

My heart pounded as Kendra stormed out. I had visions of throwing my desk chair out the window as Kendra's Mustang started up and squealed away. Our truth or dare kiss and the follow-on gropes excited, frightened, and infuriated me, combining into a feeling of nausea. Seventeen years of thinking that men would one day stir a flutter of butterflies in my stomach came into question with one kiss from my best friend. The more I tried to convince myself that the kiss was the result of a stupid game, the more I realized it was a game I wanted to play.

I laid back on my bed in hopes of stopping my world from spinning out of control. I didn't want to leave for the academy without the support of my best friend, but her accusations hurt more because of their accuracy. I hated it when she was right, and I hated that she was right about this. There was no room for gay cadets at the academy and certainly no room for gay officers in the Air Force. But there was no place I wanted to be besides the Air Force Academy.

"Knock, knock, honey." Mom interrupted with her impeccable timing.

"Not now, Mom."

"I know how hard this is, sweetheart." She came in anyway. She, too, made herself right at home on the edge of my bed. "When all my girlfriends moved away, I was sad too. You girls can write and call, and before you know it, you'll be home for Christmas and see each other again."

"Yeah, Mom. Thanks." I said what Mom needed to hear in order to feel as if she'd helped.

"Good. I'd better go start supper. I'll call you when we're ready to eat."

"Thanks, Mom."

After Mom left, I closed my burning eyes, trapping the tears that were forming. I couldn't wait until the next day when I'd be in Colorado Springs starting a new adventure at the Air Force Academy, far away from Kendra. I'd have the next six weeks of Basic Cadet Training to forget about Kendra's summary of my character.

CHAPTER 4

"Listen up, maggots. From now on, you are worth no more than this pen," yelled the upper-class Air Force Academy cadet as he held up a black Skilcraft ballpoint pen, clearly marked US Government.

"That's right. You're government property, and you will only speak when spoken to. You will limit your response to one of seven basic responses: 'yes sir, no sir, no excuse sir, sir I do not know, sir I do not understand, sir may I ask a question, or sir may I make a statement.' Do I make myself clear?"

"Yes sir," was the collective and timid reply from the fifty-four of us soon-to-be basic cadets on the Greyhound bus. We had picked up the bus from the Colorado Springs Airport, and the ride had been filled with nervous tension poorly cloaked in verbal overconfidence. All cockiness drowned the minute the bus crossed through the front gate of the academy grounds and the asshole now yelling at us climbed aboard.

"Don't whisper to me! I said, 'Do I make myself clear?'"

"YES SIR!"

"Very well. Now get your sorry asses off my bus."

Fifty-four young adults wishing we had chosen a normal college with a normal post–high school summer piled off the bus and into the screams of more upper-class dicks like the one we had just left. As I made my way off the bus, I was stunned by the imposing landscape onto which I stepped. The bus emptied onto a massive parking lot that rested at the base of an enormous ramp. The ramp ascended under a wall with tall metal letters spelling out, "BRING ME MEN." At the top of the ramp was the cadet area, on which an American flag waved against the front range of the Rocky Mountains. Almost every brochure about the academy included a photo of the cadet wing marching down the Bring Me Men ramp. The ramp was the academy's centerpiece, and the words were from a Samuel Walter Foss poem calling for people of strong character to defend the nation.

The image was iconic, and to see it with my own eyes was awe inspiring. I puffed my chest with pride. I had made it to the United States Air Force Academy. USAFA, as it was better known, was spoken as a three-syllable word, *you-SAW-fa*, as if Mr. Webster had drafted it in his first dictionary.

The upper-class pricks burst into my daydream as they made it loud and clear that once off the bus we were in the military and had better be prepared.

"Web belt. Canteen. Iodine tablet. Put one tablet in your canteen, fill it up with water, and put it on your belt," yelled Dick Number Two as other upperclassmen threw the three items at each of us.

I tried to absorb the environment, shocked that the Air Force treated its people so savagely. My rapid heartbeat pounded inside my chest, causing a pain that was only outdone by the volume with which I was required to shout out one of my seven basic responses. I was next in line to receive my three items and was pleased to see that my hurler was an attractive female upper-class cadet.

Her athletic frame filled her camouflage pants as if they had been tailored to fit her and only her. Her pants were trimmed with a dark-blue uniform belt and provided a sharp contrast to the white T-shirt tucked smoothly into her pants. Her flat stomach gave way to a robust set of tits. I could see her sports bra through the thin fabric of her T-shirt. The name Teason was positioned over her heart in blue block letters above the acronym USAFA. She wore a dark-blue beret like the other upperclassmen, and the hair I could see was short and dark brown in a fashionable cut that seemed to reveal a bolder side that straddled the fine line between the conservative military cut and a hip, trendy style.

Without thinking about where I was or what the hell I was doing, I smiled at her.

Wrong move. The upper-class cadet picked up on my small smile right away and attacked immediately. "I know you ain't smilin' at me, Basic." She shook her head. "Cadet Jackson, come take a look at my new bitch."

Another female upperclassman, Cadet Jackson presumably, came over and slowly eyed me up and down. "Well, well, Cadet Teason, what have you here?" She moved in closer, beyond acceptable civilian social limits of personal space. Cadet Jackson brought her face close to my ear, causing a reflexive head and body turn, and soon I was completely squared up with Cadet Jackson.

"Oh, no you didn't." Cadet Teason entered my personal bubble in which all three of us now resided. "Your eyes better stay right here, Basic." She used her index and middle fingers to indicate her own two deep-blue eyes.

Cadet Jackson remained at my ear into which she hissed, "You got the hots for Cadet Teason, Basic?"

"NO SIR." Shit.

This brought Cadet Jackson front and center. "What the fuck d'you just call me, Basic?"

"You better get your shit together. Think before you open your trap," Cadet Teason said.

"You haven't answered my question, Basic. I asked what the fuck you just called me." Cadet Jackson overlapped Teason.

"You ain't gonna make it one day here at my academy, Basic. You better answer Cadet Jackson," Teason spit.

"Yes ma'am," was all I could get out in between their symphony of shouts.

"What squadron are you going to, Basic?" the blur of faces in front of me asked.

"Ma'am, I do not know." This was an honest answer.

"Shit, Basic, do you know anything?" Teason yelled as she grabbed and read the five-by-seven manila cardstock dangling around my neck. She pulled it closer to her face, and the twine necklace dug into the back of my neck.

I'd be damned if I was going to give them the satisfaction of knowing they were hurting me. My pride was at stake, and without knowing this was the start of the academy's process of tearing down individual pride and rebuilding it into team pride, I stayed stoic with my eyes staring into the small space in between us.

Cadet Teason got an evil smile on her face as she read the data on my "cowbell." "Well, well, well, Basic

Cadet Eerie Cat," she mispronounced. "It seems we'll be spending the summer together, because you're in my Basic Cadet Training squadron. And if you make it through Basic Training, you'll be in my squadron for the entire year."

Shit again. How lucky was I?

"Listen up, basics," Teason yelled. "Any of you who are in the Hellcat Squadron better keep an eye on Basic Cadet Eerie Cat here." Teason twisted me by the shoulders to face the backlog of basic cadets held up by my own gender misidentification.

In the warped irony of the situation I was now in, I was turned on by the attention I was getting from this not-unattractive female cadet. I could feel the warmth and strength of her hands on my shoulders as she continued to highlight my error.

"Basic Cadet Eerie Cat has already gotten you Hellcats off to a very bad start here by not knowing a boy from a girl."

A few of my classmates snickered as they stood safely in their nervous group.

"You think that's funny, mister?" Cadet Jackson lit into the loudest and closest giggle box. "We got us a laughing man here, Cadet Teason."

Cadet Teason left my side to help Cadet Jackson dole out their next portion of shit.

They had picked a scrawny, meek boy as their next victim, easy kill, no contest. They were barely two lines into their routine when tears flowed from under his Coke-bottle glasses and over his acne-ridden face. Rather than let up, they got worse. Big surprise.

"Look at this pussy. Basic, you haven't even been here two minutes, you're bawling like a little girl, and you ain't seen nothing yet."

The young guy had reached his breaking point, albeit early on, and his shoulders shuddered with his sobs. I empathized, having recently felt the same humiliation. The two upper-class "ladies" were in his face, fogging and spraying his glasses with their insults.

For reasons unbeknownst to me, I sprinted to his side, slammed my left side against his right, and stared Cadets Teason and Jackson square in the face.

"Sir, may I ask a question?" I yelled at the top of my lungs.

After a moment that passed as fast as water froze, Cadet Teason glared at me, then dismissed me with a confused look. "Eerie Cat, go away."

"No sir." I grabbed Coke-Bottle's sweaty hand.

"What the fuck did she just call you?" a male voice from my right boomed. "Basic! You better figure out your genders before you address an upperclassman, do you understand?" a huge black man towered above me, spitting his *s*'s.

"YES MA'AM."

This brought Cadets Jackson, Teason, and my new best friend, Cadet Black Tower, front and center and into my now-shrinking space. I squeezed and released Coke-Bottle's hand, hoping that he would get away from this, but he remained glued to my side.

The three upperclassmen became red faced, and their veins popped as they spat unintelligible, crisscrossing barks. Coke-Bottle and I just stood there together, braving the winds, knowing that we'd made a name for ourselves early on. This was a great start to the first part of Basic Cadet Training, also known as BCT, or affectionately referred to and pronounced as First Beast.

When the three upperclassmen ran out of breath and insults, they let us go and began to prey on the horde of basic cadets behind us.

We moved on through the line with great relief, compliantly putting an iodine tablet and water in our canteens and our canteens on our web belts.

I had barely put the filled canteen onto my web belt when more standard USAFA gear came flying my way. The onslaught included one green laundry bag, five white T-shirts, five pairs of blue shorts, five pairs of white crew-length socks, one bottle of Prell shampoo, one bar of Ivory soap, one solid stick of Secret deodorant, and a pocket-sized book that I presumed to be a Bible. There was no time to sort or recognize anything. Everything that was thrown at me went right into the green bag except for the little book, which we were quickly informed was titled *Contrails*, a condensed book of required knowledge. So it was a bible of sorts. It was the word according to USAFA with USAFA heritage information, USAFA quotes, and various details of USAFA life. As dutiful disciples of the "word," we were to memorize it word for word.

I held my *Contrails* book in front of my face while at the position of attention as we were instructed to do any time we were standing still. My eyes moved over the words on the page, but there was no comprehension of those words and certainly no retention of those words. Lines of basic cadets were herded through an indoor labyrinth of halls and rooms, blindly following an endless array of upper-class escorts. We had forfeited our watches on the bus and had no idea what time it was or if it was even still daytime. It didn't really matter anyway since we were no longer in control of our schedules.

As we stood in silence reading our *Contrails*, our line slowly disappeared into another one of the many rooms we had been cycled through that day. Using my peripheral vision, I could see the basic cadets coming out of the room had less hair than those that went in. Ever the perceptive one, I discerned that we were in line for the hairdresser. As the line crept closer to the room, multiple pairs of trimmers buzzed, and chatty conversation filled the otherwise silent air.

I kept my *Contrails* close to my face, but my focus was on the activity in the room, not the words on the page. The five hairdressers stood behind their barbershop chairs that did not discriminate based on gender. The clippers that shaved the men bald were the same ones that gave each woman an identical blunt pixie cut.

I continued to stand at attention with the book in front of my face even inside the barbershop, and a cute soon-to-be pixie dragged my attention away from the words on the page. She sat in the middle chair and was chatting with her short, Asian hairdresser as if she were in the middle of a spa day and were paying for her hair to be butchered without any regard to current hairstyle trends. I slid my *Contrails* to the side ever so slightly so I could watch this woman smile and laugh with her hairdresser.

"So, I guess I don't really have a say in what I want, huh?" Pixie Girl said.

Her butcher shook her head no and commenced chopping away at Pixie's dry, shoulder-length hair.

Her lighthearted banter brought calmness to the room and made everyone else a little more relaxed. I was mesmerized by her casual, carefree energy, like she had no idea what Basic Cadet Training entailed. I was drawn to her affable nature found within the jungle of otherwise wild beasts.

She looked over at me, and as we locked eyes for the briefest of moments, I got a flutter in my stomach as if I had just met a celebrity. I didn't know if it was the altitude, the exhaustion of the first day of Basic Cadet Training, or the sadistic pleasure I got from the recent Cadet Teason tongue lashing, but the God who abhorred gayness was certainly leading a lot of same-sex temptation into my daily bread.

I immediately moved the *Contrails* back in front of my face, hoping she didn't think I was staring at her.

"Hey, you can put your book down in here," Pixie Girl said.

I slid the book to the side again to see that she was still looking at me. I glanced to my left and right to see that I was the only one in there standing at attention with my book in front of my face. My face felt hot as I let my lips curve into a sheepish smile. I put the book in my pocket and stretched my back, which wasn't used to my standing up straight for so long.

"I'm Basic Cadet Roberts to the upper-class goons but Mandy to you."

"Lex," I said, still in disbelief at how casual this woman was about the day we'd been through thus far. The guys on either side of her were getting shaved right down to their bleach-white scalps while she was getting a haircut that would get a barber dis-barbered and she was trying to have a conversation with me.

Her barber skipped the normal routine of checking to see if the left- and right-side lengths matched and indicated that the haircut was complete by removing the smock. The smock had been hiding Mandy's cowbell, which had an H-C, which stood for Hellcat squadron, Charlie flight.

"Hey, we'll be Hellcats together this summer." Mandy shook out her thick, brown pixie hairdo while eyeing my cowbell that read H-D, which meant I was in the same squadron but in a different flight.

Mandy quickly informed me that the forty academic-year squadrons were reduced to only ten Basic Cadet Training squadrons, labeled A through J, during the summers. Of course, just being labeled as an alphabet letter wasn't sufficient enough for a military school, so the A squadron were Aggressors, B stood for Barbarians, on down to us Hellcats.

Mandy's voice continued to bubble on about the summer alphabet squadrons and their four flights, each somehow corresponding to the forty academic-year numbered squadrons. It clearly made sense to her, but the explanation sailed right over my head.

The bottom line boomeranged. "So we'll be together this summer and then living on the same floor during the school year. Of course, we won't be able to cross that invisible line between our school year squadrons, but I'll be nearby if you need me," Mandy concluded. The invisible line existed for the sole purpose of keeping freshmen in the geographic confines of their own squadron.

Not knowing how she knew all this, I was just relieved that I was going to be spending the summer with someone who could shed some light on my lack of awareness.

The day continued to blur on until the mass of 1,162 basic cadets was inside some auditorium.

"Listen up, basics," the upperclassman on stage boomed. His chiseled body showed through his tailored T-shirt. Talk about poster child for military recruiting. The inappropriate thoughts I was having about this fine specimen of a man would challenge Kendra's accusations of my sexual orientation.

"You all have been through a lot today, and it's only going to get worse as the summer goes on," Cadet Chiseled Chest bellowed. He was the first person to talk to us as if we were human. "So, knowing what you know now, you better decide real soon if you're gonna commit the next four years of your life to the United States Air Force Academy or run home to your mommas."

Run home? Hell no. I was right where I wanted to be. Granted, the day had been a bit stressful, but I was proud of myself, and I'd never been surer that where I was at was where I intended to be.

"One thing you better get straight, and I mean straight, is that there ain't no room for faggots here." His voice quickly changed into a Southern drawl that indicated he was a good ol' boy speaking from his soul and not from a memorized speech. "There's exactly one thousand, one hundred and sixty-two of you in here. Chances are, 'bout a hunnert of y'all are homos. So take a look to your left and right, you probably got a fag or lez sitting right next to you."

I swore that guy was looking right at me when he said lez. The stress of the day and what I'd put myself into became very apparent. If my feelings for Kendra were just isolated feelings for her, I could work past that. If my feelings for Kendra were indicative of how I felt for other women, then I had a much bigger problem. My earlier interaction with Cadet Teason and then the butterflies released by Pixie Girl Mandy led me to believe I had the bigger problem.

God damn Kendra! I was furious that she had put this shit into my head. I wanted to pummel the crap out of her, I wanted to yell at her, I wanted to cry to her, I wanted to talk to her. Instead, I sat there at attention with my eyes fixed on our speaker. My head was flooded with a thousand thoughts: Kendra, our friendship, our kiss, this school, this summer, and my future. The shit I thought I could figure out after I got away from Kendra overwhelmed me, and I knew there'd be no time in the next six weeks to sort it out.

It was right there in that auditorium, surrounded by 1,161 other sweaty, frightened basic cadets that I became determined to find a straight and narrow pathway until graduating from the academy. Cadet Chiseled Chest continued on with his southern drawl sermon, but I caught none of it. I was too busy figuring out how to convert the feelings I got from Kendra or, hell, from any woman, into the feelings I should be getting from men.

CHAPTER 5

Later, when we were separated into squadrons and marched to our rooms, I was surprised to see that it was still daytime. The sun was just above the peak of the Rocky Mountain range that cradled the academy grounds, which indicated it must be late afternoon going on evening. Of course none of it mattered since the upperclassmen owned us and dictated our schedules for the next six weeks.

A random upperclassman directed me to my room, and I was surprised at how crowded the room seemed. There were three massive bed assemblies in the small room. Each bed unit had a full-sized mattress that served as a roof over a large desk with a locking computer cabinet. A narrow wooden ladder slanted slightly against the unit to allow ascension into bed without being a tripping hazard on the ground. The wall to the left of the doorway hosted two closets, and the sidewall to the right of the doorway had a wide counter and sink with mirrored medicine cabinets above it and cabinet space below. Two bed units would have fit the room perfectly, but the third one was a definite afterthought as a solution to maximizing space. Opposite the doorway was a wall-to-wall window that went from mid-thigh to the ceiling. The window overlooked a parking lot, the enormous athletic complex, and about five football fields.

"Don't mind me," came a voice from between the bed unit and the window. A skinny, curly-haired blonde girl lay on her stomach with an ankle in each hand rocking back and forth. If the shock of an unexpected voice didn't scare me, the sight of my roommate did.

"I got bad gas, so I gotta do these fart flops," the belly rocker said. A rapid and loud whoosh of air came from her backside. "See? Feels so much better."

Belly Rocker popped to her feet and stuck out a hand. "I'm Paige Seivers."

I shook the extended hand but was still in a bit of shock since I couldn't imagine rocking farts out of my system, let alone rocking farts out of my system without some advanced degree of privacy.

"I had to hide behind the bed since we can't shut the door unless we're changing, and I didn't want to do my fart flops naked. That'd be a little awkward,"

Paige said.

Yeah, doing it with clothes on made it normal.

"So what's your name?"

"Oh, sorry. Alexis."

"Well, nice to meet you. I'm not sure if we're getting a third roommate, but I guess we got the space if she shows up. I hope you don't mind, but I took the bed closest to the sink."

I wasn't sure if Paige had gone through the same mind-spinning first day as me because she talked as if we were on day one of summer camp.

"EERIE CAT," a female voice, unmistakably and unforgettably Cadet Teason's, hollered from down the hallway.

"Shit," I mumbled.

"Is that you?" Paige asked.

I nodded.

"Eeeerie Cat." The voice mimicked a sweet, singsong voice and was very close to finding the right room.

"You better get out there," Paige said.

I got myself to the doorway of the room and shouted, "Yes ma'am."

"Eerie Cat, get over here." Cadet Teason pointed to a spot against the wall, right in front of her. I did my best facing movements, pivoting on my outside foot every time I made a ninety-degree turn. We'd only had a quick crash course on how we were supposed to walk for the next year, but it was enough to get me out in the hallway. I stood in front of Cadet Teason, very aware that my classmates were staring from their rooms, too afraid to come out.

Cadet Teason slammed her right palm flat against the wall, right next to my left ear.

"You having a good first day, Eerie Cat?"

"Yes ma'am." I matched the same low volume with which Cadet Teason spoke.

"Don't whisper to me, Eerie Cat. I ain't your girlfriend," Cadet Teason hissed.

"NO MA'AM," I shouted in direct conflict with the quick enjoyment I got from the thought of having her make us into a couple.

Cadet Teason leaned in on her extended right arm, bringing her mouth disturbingly close to my right ear.

I was cornered, out of control, and very uncomfortable. My back was stiff and against the wall, trapped on the left side by Cadet Teason's right arm and trapped on the right by Cadet Teason's face. I knew from earlier that day that my gaze had to stay straight ahead, which left me staring at the right side of Cadet Teason's face. Her face was so close that I couldn't help but notice the strawberry smell of her hair and how this forbidden fruit of a drill sergeant was inexplicably turning me on.

What the hell was wrong with me?

"That was a very impressive show of teamwork you put on this morning, Erecat," Cadet Teason's voice was barely a whisper as she pronounced my name correctly.

Well, the hell that was wrong with me was this tempting forbidden fruit.

"You're catching on real quick to what this place is about. I got my eye on you, so you better not disappoint me. Understand?"

"YES MA'AM!" I yelled right into Cadet Teason's ear. It was the only way I could think of to get her away from me, even though deep inside I wanted to be near her.

"Damn, Eerie Cat, what the fuck was that for?" Cadet Teason recoiled and stuck her finger in her ear, shaking it in hopes of regaining some of her hearing.

I bit the insides of my cheeks to keep from laughing out loud. "Ma'am, I do not know," I shouted.

"Get out of here Eerie Cat, I'm watching you."

I bolted back to the room where Paige waited for the backstory. But before I could explain, I smiled as I heard other upper-class cadets out in the hallway laughing at Cadet Teason, who muttered, "Little shit."

My mental scoreboard tallied Eerie Cat 1, Academy 0. A small victory that felt enormous.

CHAPTER 6

"Out in the hallway, basics!" could barely be heard over the clanging of garbage cans and Guns N' Roses' "Welcome to the Jungle" blaring through two large speakers stretched out into the hallway.

"What time is it?" I groaned from my elevated bed.

"Who knows? But you know we're in for a treat with these guys." Paige was already dressed in her issued blue shorts and white T-shirt. She was an obvious cheerful, morning person as she looked up and told me to "get moving, sleepyhead." She would have to be killed for her five a.m. optimism, but there was no time for murder.

"You basics are making me late!" yelled an upperclassman.

"PT gear, let's go," yelled another.

We flowed out into the hallway frightened and tired, two feelings that would compete for dominance over the next six weeks. Once the upperclassmen were satisfied that all their charges were assembled, they marched the Hellcat squadron of basic cadets out with the other nine basic cadet squadrons onto a cold, wet open field for physical training, or PT.

The cadre of upperclassmen who abused us through this training only saw us as basic cadets, not as the recruited all-state, sports team captains that most of us were. This morning they ran us through stretches, sprints, runs, push-ups, and sit-ups. Even those of us who arrived at the academy in the very best of shape were gasping for what little air was offered up at 7,258 feet above sea level. For the most part, we survived. Some left stomach contents at various places on the field. Most had cramping muscles of some sort. All were glad it was over.

Once off the PT field, we were ordered into bathrobes and flip-flops and herded to the showers like slaughterhouse cattle. Any embarrassment suffered from poor athletic performance on the field was replaced by an even higher degree of humiliation brought on by immodest communal showers, proctored by an upperclassman armed with a piercing whistle.

The whistle replaced shouts from upper-class cadets as the latest form of command we were to obey as the obedient cows we were fast becoming.

Each tweet of the whistle meant we were to cycle to the next showerhead. As if responding to a whistle wasn't demeaning enough, the fact that every female Hellcat basic cadet was bare-ass naked in the shower room made it clear that modesty went out with our now distant memories of leisurely bubble baths.

"Fifteen seconds, basics. That's it," said Cadet Whistle Tweeter.

Tweet. Shuffling flip-flops. Fifteen seconds pass. Tweet. Shuffling flip-flops. Repeat. "Double up. You all are taking entirely too long!" Tweet. Shuffling flip-flops.

Kendra would have predicted that the thought of showering with seven naked Air Force Academy women would arouse me. But the circumstances surrounding this shared shower scene were less than ideal and definitely not anticipated. Sure I was surrounded by fit, athletic, type-A, motivated women. But a communal shower run by a dictatorial whistle blower made any pre-fantasy thoughts of hot, steamy, sexy shower scenes obliterate into an asexual world. The showers were hardly the place for meeting and greeting, especially considering the fifteen-second time constraint. Hardly enough time to dole out a pickup line. Or get clean. Some women were cutting ahead in line and taking their own sweet time in the showers. They were obviously the upper-class beast masters.

Tweet. Time for me to shuffle my flip-flops. There were six open stalls, three to the left and three to the right with one common drain in the middle. Peeing in the shower was out of the question. The thought of a solitary yellow trail streaming from one of the stalls into the shared drain made me smile, on the inside of course. Considering our dehydrated states, the piss would be dark yellow and give off the foulest stench, making it an easy trail to follow back to the culprit. God help the newbie with the small bladder. I could only imagine the hell she would get from the beast masters. Right then and there, I decided to hold it for the next four years.

At least I had something to occupy my mind besides the fact that I was butt naked and about to take my first multiparty shower. I went all the way to the back left stall where another basic cadet was taking more than her allotted fifteen seconds. I wasn't going to lose out on my fifteen seconds of spray so in an effort to get wet, I nudged her a bit. As I drenched my hair, our bodies touched, and I felt the girl's rigid tits bookending my right shoulder blade. Mission accomplished, I was wet.

"Get in a stall with your own classmate, basic." The voice was loud, the voice was near, and the voice was Cadet Teason, right there in the stall with me. Mission complete, I was humiliated.

I forfeited my remaining seconds before the whistle blew again and quickly shuffled out of the shower into the changing area where I toweled off and threw on my robe. I scurried back to my room and got dressed with a few minutes of closed door time to spare before Paige returned.

I sat on the floor staring out the window trying to digest my latest blunder. I couldn't get Cadet Teason's body out of my mind. In the brief embarrassing shower we shared, I had noticed Teason's six pack stomach and muscular arms. There was no forgetting the feel of her tits against my shoulder. I tried to imagine the taste of one of those perfect tits but the only flavor that surfaced was the recollection of Kendra's breast in my mouth. That snapped me back to reality and made my mouth fill with the same puke-predicting saliva Kendra had brought out.

This had to be one of God's cruel tests the nuns had always warned us about. Cadet Teason had been put into my life to test my resolve of staying focused on my academy goal.

Lex, your attraction to Cadet Teason is just a deep-felt respect, I tried to convince myself.

It was deep all right.

CHAPTER 7

"Dude, you seen the rack on Teason?" Pipes whispered. Basic Cadet Piperata was one of the six of us huddled together over a shared tin of shoe polish as we shined our boots. The simple acts of sitting down and shutting the doors to our rooms were common privileges that had been taken away from us as lowly basic cadets but would be given back to us as luxuries after BCT. So we all stood around the computer desk bullshitting. The forty-five minutes of Individual Cadet Time, or ICT, that we got each night was a precious treat during which we weren't yelled at and weren't expected to spout quotes from historical military leaders. Twice a week, I spent my ICT writing a letter home as any dutiful daughter should, but the other five days of ICT were filled with bonding time with my new best friends.

"No shit, man. She's cut." Apparently, chivalry was dead as the four guys talked openly but quietly about Cadet Teason in front of Paige and me. Not that I cared. My only beef was that I couldn't share my shower story with them. That would have sent them over the edge.

"What I wouldn't give to…" words lost necessity as Pipes grabbed the invisible woman in front of him and thrust himself back and forth inside her.

"Daniel Piperata, you should be ashamed of yourself." Paige was turning out to be quite the mother figure for all of us.

"Sorry, Paige. Maybe I should be focusing on the sure thing." Pipes turned toward her and tried to grab her very real hips as he continued thrusting himself into the air.

"Pipes!" Paige squealed. "Stop!"

The six of us all laughed, knowing full well that Pipes would never try anything with Paige or me. Where Paige was the mother, Pipes was our overprotective big brother. As an only child, I liked having someone look over me like Pipes did.

"What the fuck is going on in here?"

We all snapped to attention, dropping boots and the tin of shoe polish as we stared at Cadet Tollet, who was now inside our room.

"Apparently, we need to put more saltpeter in your food, Piperata." Cadet Tollet had just propagated the old wives' tale that the academy allegedly put saltpeter in the mess hall food to help control our amorous natures.

"No sir. We were just…I was just…Sir may I make a statement?" We were all shaking with silent laughter as Pipes, our usually suave and composed classmate, struggled to explain his thrusting to Cadet Tollet.

"No, you may not make a statement." Cadet Tollet turned out into the hallway.

We relaxed and laughed at Pipes until we heard Cadet Tollet again. "All male D-Flight Hellcat basics, out in the hallway now."

Thirty young men filed out into the hallway and only four of them knew why.

Cadet Tollet lined our male classmates along the two facing hallway walls, fifteen per side. He paced the middle of the hallway. "It seems that Basic Cadet Piperata has not been challenged by Basic Cadet Training and has enough energy to go after one of your female classmates in order to satisfy his sexual needs. Since all of you are a team, you will all help Piperata expend his sexual energies. Piperata, front and center."

We watched Pipes nervously run in front of our male classmates. At Cadet Tollet's request, Pipes demonstrated the pelvic thrusts he had jokingly aimed at Paige only minutes earlier.

"You will all continue the Piperata motion while shouting, 'My name is Basic Cadet Piperata and I want to GET SOME!' Is this clear?"

"Yes sir."

"Begin."

From our room, Paige and I could only see half the group awkwardly thrusting their hips forward while shouting. Their facial expressions displayed a conflict between thinking this was a joke and being utterly humiliated. But they were a team and, after a few nervous repetitions of the chant-and-thrust routine, were doing it in perfect harmony. The coordinated chant increased in volume, which brought out the rest of the upper-class team. They acted appalled at the thrusting and began a high-volumed criticism of the men's blatant disregard for women.

This was all part of the goal of basic training: to rebuild broken-down individuals into a cohesive team. The irony was that the breaking down happened by the same cadre working to build us up together.

Paige and I watched helplessly as the guys tried to shout back answers to the barrage of questions, and when they tried to stop thrusting out of "respect for the female gender" they were again scolded for not obeying the order to thrust. It was yet another aspect of the basic training agenda: there was no right answer, anything we did was wrong.

Since there was no right, we ran out into the hallway with our hastily thought-out plan. We literally pushed upperclassmen aside until we were in the middle of the hallway, in the center of the two lines of our chanting, thrusting male classmates. We started thrusting much more actively than Pipes had done when he first started this mess. Together, Paige and I chanted, "We want some too."

After only a couple stanzas of our song, we were the only ones chanting and the only ones thrusting. Soon, a circle of upperclassmen surrounded us, bringing our thrusting to a halt. I was beginning to think that we had made a big mistake, but when one upperclassman busted out laughing, the rest of them went down in laughter, too, and we were all quickly sent back to our rooms. Yet another small victory over seemingly senseless academy games.

CHAPTER 8

Life went on as normal for the next couple weeks, at least the normal to which we were quickly assimilating: five a.m. workouts, fifteen-second showers, constantly being yelled at and not being able to close our bedroom doors. This was life as a basic cadet at the academy, and this was the life I had chosen for myself. Twenty-three days after we had set foot on the academy proper, we were packing up to hike out to another part of the campus.

The three-mile hike out to Jack's Valley was exciting because we were headed out for the unknown series of challenges of Second Beast, the field training portion of Basic Cadet Training. The challenges up until Jack's Valley had been primarily mental ones: memorizing quotes, putting the team before your own needs or pains, and playing the game of never being right. Second Beast promised a camping-type atmosphere with an assault course, confidence course, leadership reaction course, and tear-gas tent, culminating with a pugil-stick competition that would crown the winner big bad basic. These were the activities more suited to my tomboy demeanor.

The hike out to Jack's Valley went quickly, but my pre-departure and en route drinks ensured I was over hydrated with a bladder about to burst. Therefore, my first anxiously anticipated stop in Jack's Valley was the latrine. I was shocked to see the toilet facilities were set up with as much privacy as prison facilities. The latrine consisted of two elevated rows of five toilets inside a large canvas tent. The two rows were back-to-back and separated by a hanging piece of canvas. The five toilets were side-by-side and separated only by a roll of toilet paper suspended by a metal bar from the top of the tent.

First the showers and now the toilets. This was a huge obstacle for a modest girl from the East. I would have rather taken four more years' worth of shared showers than one pee next to someone. An Air Force that so openly condemned homosexual behavior and yet provided such opportunities for exposure on every level never ceased to amaze me. Fortunately, I was the only one in there, so I quickly sat myself, party of one, at the toilet for ten. The next thirteen days in Jack's Valley proved to be a mental puzzle of timing my water consumption so my body could drain itself during the toilets' lower turnout periods.

Our sleeping accommodations were large canvas tents, larger than the toilet tent, lest any of us get them confused. Since the tents weren't coed, all the G squadron, or Grim Reapers, and Hellcat female basic cadets shared one tent. Fitting sixteen of us in there was a tight fit, but our cots were narrow, and I presumed that the physical proximity held a deeper psychological intent of bringing us closer as a class.

Since Paige and I already got along well, we took cots next to each other. She had fast become my beast buddy, taking care of me by keeping my perspective focused on the "game" of Basic Cadet Training. I was thrilled to see Mandy, the Pixie Girl I had met in the barber shop on day one, take a cot position on the other side of me. I was enveloped by two positive energies who didn't take Beast seriously enough to let it stress them out.

The first night in Jack's Valley, Paige sat cross-legged in between Mandy's and my cot. She held her flashlight under her chin like she was going to tell a ghost story.

"Okay, Mandy, why did you want to come to the academy?" Paige asked.

Paige moved the flashlight and held it under Mandy's chin so she could give her answer.

"Because someone told me I couldn't get in."

It was a simple answer, and I appreciated it because it was similar to my reasons for being at the academy: wanting something that was difficult to achieve, wanting to do something that few people could say they'd done.

The flashlight shone up from Paige's chin again. "Lex, if you could hook up with any upperclassman, who would it be?"

I was shocked at the change in tone from the question Mandy got to the one posed to me. Of course, Cadet Teason came to mind, but only because she was the last person about whom I remembered having any lustful thoughts. I tried to quickly come up with the name of a male upperclassman but all names but Teason escaped me.

"It can be male or female," Paige clarified.

The flashlight under my chin now became warm and started a sweat in my body despite the cool temps up at seven thousand–some-odd feet in Colorado.

"SIEVERS!" hissed an upper-class intrusion, welcomed by me more than anyone. The head that popped through the thick canvas tent flap was accompanied by a flashlight-wielding hand that put Paige in the spotlight. "Get back in your rack and go to sleep!" The spotlight flicked back and forth between Mandy and me, and the voice reprimanded in a pissed-off whisper, "You too, Roberts and Erecat."

The three of us lay back on our cots, laughing at our minor scolding.

"I still want to know your answer, Lex," Paige whispered. If not for the follow-on "male or female" question clarification, I would have thought Paige to be the ditzy, be-bopping soul she came across as being. The unanswered question made me think that Paige was an intuitive being who would have to be watched carefully.

"Me too," said Mandy. She would have to be watched as well.

I pretended to fall asleep quicker than I could reply and let them be the last ones to speak until the morning.

CHAPTER 9

"Lex, let's go." Paige's bubbly whisper woke me up before our upper-class alarm clocks went off. The early wake-up and the first wake-up in Jack's Valley caused a little bit of confusion on my part as I struggled to figure out why I was waking up in a tent, and with Paige and Mandy standing by my head.

"Come on, modest girl, let's get to the toilet tent before anyone else." It was perceptive comments like that from Paige that confirmed my thoughts from the night prior that she was one to keep an eye on.

The three of us jogged to the toilet tent, and Paige served as the toilet tent maître d', "Mandy, you and me on the right." This freed up the entire row of five toilets for my private selection and use. We jogged back to the tent where our tentmates were still sleeping. Our early awakenings gave us ample time to get ready before the chaos of the upper-class wake-ups, and not being rushed was a peaceful way to prepare for the day's challenges.

The shirt tuck was another morning ritual Paige and I had that started during First Beast. The military way of tucking in your shirt was further tightening an already tucked-in shirt. Paige had the self-tuck down to a science as she would lean back, grab any shirt slack from her left and right sides, fold it back and tuck the fold into her pants. Once she had tucked in her own shirt, she would pull me backward by my shoulders, grab my shirt side slack, fold it back and tuck it in. She would finish by putting both her thumbs inside my waistband right at my belly button, then run her thumbs backward to smooth out any shirt wrinkles. Paige had done this each morning with the same matter-of-fact manner a mother would lick her palms and smooth down her child's cowlick. She seemed to welcome her role as the caregiver as much as I appreciated being cared for.

Paige brought Mandy in on our shirt-tuck routine after she finished my shirt. "Lex, give Mandy a tuck."

Mandy obediently turned her back to me, and I grabbed her shoulders to get her to lean back. The feel of her strong shoulders in my hands sent shocks through my body. The electricity of touching her pulled my skin up into involuntary goose bumps. I stood there dumbfounded by the sensations caused by the rapid-fire, non-platonic thoughts about Mandy shooting through my head.

My hands moved in slow motion as I tried to settle the debate of what felt more natural: my illegal attraction to the woman under my hands or suppressing the attraction to the woman under my hands.

"You need me to finish?" Paige tried to speed up the process with her rhetorical question.

My shaky hands continued what I had barely started as I tucked in the sides of Mandy's shirt. My mind transitioned movements into slow motion as I reached my hands around Mandy to begin the final step of the tuck. My hands followed Mandy's hard stomach until they grazed her belly button protruding ever so slightly from her flat stomach. I dipped my thumbs below her waistband, suddenly very paranoid of my breath on her neck. My thumbs chased shirt wrinkles back toward the shirt folds where my hands tucked them in one last time.

Taking advantage of the opportunity the tuck afforded, I put the palms of my hands on Mandy's sides and ran them backward to unnecessarily smooth out invisible wrinkles. "All done."

"Great. Thanks." Mandy turned to face me. There were goose bumps on her arms and two on her chest, and it was obvious that I noticed.

I turned around as if a 180-degree turn would transport me somewhere else. But I just ran into Paige, who saved Mandy and me from any explanation by telling us it was time to wake up our "lazy tentmates."

The three of us helped get our tentmates up and moving. We straightened up cots and sleeping bags while the rest of the girls took their sweet time wiping the dirt-laden sleep from their eyes and getting dressed for the adventures of Second Beast. And what an adventure it was!

On our first day, we went through the obstacle course, where we wedged our bodies between barbed wire and pea gravel, sprinted across a thin balance beam perched above a mud pit, and scaled a thick-roped cargo net to a narrow platform forty feet above the ground. The shared misery of Basic Training's physical challenges propelled me to the obstacle's pinnacle. It wasn't until I had fully ascended the peak that I remembered I was afraid of heights. The view from forty feet above my latest victory was short lived and ruined by the upper-class cadet who ruled the forty-foot roost.

"Basic! What are you gazing at?" yelled the destroyer of my moment.

I had enough time to register that she was cute and blonde but enough sense to remember that she was still an upperclassman. What I failed to have had the sense to remember were the instructions given at the bottom of the cargo net, namely to scale the net, slide on your belly across the narrow platform, and descend the cargo net on the opposite side. This was for our safety and for academy's liability I'm sure. Well, they shouldn't have put a cute blonde at the top.

I began to stand up at attention since that was the courtesy rendered to an upperclassman, especially a cute blonde one. Not a smart move on my part.

Or maybe it was.

Cadet Cute Blonde swiftly arrested my upward movement with a downward pull to the narrow platform. Her firm grip around my waist was the closest thing to affection I'd had since I'd set foot on the academy grounds. Our labored breathing was synchronized and with a quiet, caring tone she asked, "Are you okay?"

"Yes ma'am," I replied with the same softness in my voice. I pulled back from our embrace slightly to give her the same smile I had given Cadet Teason on day one of First Beast. Clearly, I didn't learn the lesson from that day.

"Are you kidding me?" she yelled. "Scale up, slide across." She repeated the instructions we had gotten on the ground.

"Yes ma'am!"

With her arm of safety still snug around my waist, she guided me across her platform and got me to the descending side of the obstacle. I began my controlled tumble to the ground but not without one last upward gaze to the platform. I smiled again when Cadet Cute Blonde stared down at me, winked, and smiled.

I loved the physical contact that Jack's Valley and Second Beast afforded. Not only did the physical nature match my natural athletic abilities, it also matched my desire for women that had been dormant until Kendra's truth or dare kiss.

Because the male upperclassmen were careful about the degree of physical contact with female basic cadets, physical "corrections" made on females were made by females. That was fine by me. Hugging a cute blonde in the middle of the obstacle course didn't faze me. Having the attention of a female upperclasswoman grabbing my helmet on the assault course, pulling our bodies closer together so she could yell at me didn't faze me. I enjoyed it, and I wondered if I didn't invite it.

"Eerie Cat, I swear you bring this shit on yourself," yelled Cadet Helmet Grabber one day on the assault course.

"No ma'am," I yelled back. *Think what you want, woman. I can feel the heat of your skin and the warmth of your breath.* My self-confidence in my attraction to females caught me off guard but never during the interaction, always after. What didn't catch me off guard was the interaction and subsequent attraction felt comforting, as if there were no other emotion to feel.

No matter what, despite being tough, Jack's Valley was a blast. The completion of the hike back from Jack's meant two major things: our acceptance into the wing and Doolie Day Out.

The Acceptance Parade was the official recognition of our graduation from Basic Cadet Training and our promotion from the rank of basic cadet to cadet fourth class. In order to further distance itself from a civilian college, academy classes weren't referred to as freshman through senior. A senior was called a firstie, a junior was a two degree, and a sophomore was a three degree. The civilian sector would call us freshmen, but this was no ordinary college, so you never heard anyone label themselves as freshmen.

As fourth-class cadets, we might be called four degrees, but we were also known as doolies or SMACKs, an acronym for Soldier, Minus Ability, Coordination, and Knowledge. SMACK was the preferred moniker, and as SMACKs we had graduated to a life status where we could close our doors and sit down when we were in our rooms.

The Acceptance Parade was full of the pomp and circumstance one would expect from the military, and I was a sucker for pomp and circumstance. Several families filled the parade-ground stands to watch, and their spectatorship brought USAFA's other pet name, The Zoo, to life. As the Zoo's newest attraction, we ate up the attention, marching in a forty-flight wedge toward the main body of the cadet wing, thereby officially entering our academic-year cadet squadrons.

I allowed myself the small pleasure and amusement of the Acceptance Parade being my celebration of making it through the academy's six-week homophobic program. I had enjoyed the attention of a few women. Although nothing had happened between me and Cadet Teason, Mandy, or the blonde on the obstacle course, I had experienced an awakening.

CHAPTER 10

The day after our acceptance into the wing, we got ready to leave the academy grounds for the first time. The cadet sponsor program enlisted the hospitality of local families in the Colorado Springs community, who opened up their homes to cadets to provide downtime, home-cooked meals, and time away from the academy. Each cadet was paired with a sponsor family, and this would be our first meeting with our new families. We would get an entire afternoon and evening away from the academy, our first extended opportunity to lounge around and our first chance to make a phone call. Yet another example of looking forward to a luxury that had once been an assumed aspect of life.

"What's the name of your family?" Paige threw physical training gear into a laundry bag that doubled as a duffel bag.

On my sponsor family information card, the name that had been typed on there was crossed out and another name penned in. "Ms. Henrietta Heiser."

"My family has a labrador and an eighteen-year-old son," Paige read. "Hope he's cute."

"The labrador or the son?" I joked.

"Ha ha. What's it say about your family?"

"Nothing. My previous family was a husband and wife. My new sponsor is apparently an old spinster who wants me to rub her bunions." I honestly didn't care if that was the case. All I really wanted to do was lie on a bed and listen to music with no fear of having to pop to attention if some upperclassman decided he wanted to hear Major General John M. Schofield's graduation address to the graduating class of 1879 at West Point, which was exactly how we were expected to preface the ninety-word quote.

"Well, have fun." Paige squared the corner in front of our door.

I followed Paige down to the base of the Bring Me Men ramp and waited for Ms. Heiser by the stone pillar with the cardboard sign with an "H."

No more than ten minutes later, a mellow-yellow convertible Mustang pulled up with the top down and music blaring from the car's sound system. The driver, with her spiked brunette hair bleached at the tips, stood out as much as her car in contrast to the plump schoolmarms and balding PTA fathers in their minivans. The deafening boom of the bass was cut off as the driver flipped off the ignition and jumped out. She pushed blue-framed Oakley sunglasses up onto the top of her head as she walked right up to me. "Alexis?"

"Yes ma'am."

"Well let's go, hon." Ms. Heiser's voice was raspy enough to be charged $1.99 a minute to listen to but not raspy enough to pass for a smoker. She grabbed my laundry bag, threw it in the back seat, and slid into the driver's seat.

I sat shotgun and noticed Ms. Heiser's long golden legs. As she depressed the clutch and started the car, you could see her leg muscles crying for something more demanding than pushing skinny little car pedals. Within seconds, I felt the bold purr of the Mustang as the raspy, husky harmonies of two women singing "Closer to Fine" picked up right where they had left off as we zoomed out of the parking lot.

Ms. Heiser didn't say a word during the twenty-minute drive into downtown Colorado Springs. Frankly, I didn't care, because the windy ride away from the academy was a literal breath of fresh air.

"Welcome to my humble abode." Ms. Heiser pulled the Mustang into the last driveway in a row of gorgeous custom homes. She held the front door open as I took in the sights of her house nestled in the Rocky Mountain foothills. "You like it?" she asked as we entered.

"Wow. Yeah. Yes ma'am. It's amazing." There were no words to describe the impact of her generous lot of land or the stunning view from her house.

"All right. For starters, no 'ma'am' here. Everyone calls me Henry." She winked. "You can chill out here, okay? You've earned it. This is your time to relax, so I'll give you the quick tour, and then the rest of the day is yours.

"I designed this house, and after I got this particular lot, I found out that zoning laws wouldn't allow any more building past here, so I added more windows to overlook the north and entire east sides of the house."

"I love how open it is. You can't tell where the kitchen ends and this huge living room begins." My mouth hung open while I dragged my fingers along the cool granite countertop of the kitchen island, staring up at the Rampart Mountain Range. "That fireplace looks like it belongs in a ski lodge!" I walked into the family room.

"That's precisely where I got the idea from," Henry said. "And you'll love this." She touched the huge dimpled copper kettle that hung from a black wrought-iron hook in the fireplace boulders. "I keep it stocked with water, and when I have a fire going, it heats it up just right for hot chocolate."

"Why would you stay in here drinking hot cocoa when you could be out there in that?" I accelerated the tour as I pointed through the sliding glass door at the steaming hot tub on the redwood deck.

"Go on out there. The view gets better."

I stepped out onto the deck that was only six feet wide but ran the length of the house. I peeked through a pair of French doors at the end of the deck past the hot tub. The room had a tall king-sized bed, a six-drawer oak dresser, and a smaller stone fireplace. When I realized this was Henry's bedroom, I jumped back from the glass. "Sorry, I'm getting nosy."

"That's okay. I'm glad someone appreciates my home. I put a lot of thought into this place. Check this out." Henry opened the doors to her bedroom and walked to the fireplace. She reached into the fireplace, grabbed an iron handle, and pivoted an iron plate on the bottom of the fireplace. As the plate pivoted clockwise, a vertical iron wall came into view and created a new back wall. "See, this fireplace shares the chimney with the big one in the living room so if I have a fire going in there and then decide to go to bed, I just rotate the fire into my bedroom." Henry smiled a victorious smile.

"What'd you do, win the lottery? This place is fantastic!" Apparently, I was still being nosy.

"Something like that."

My eyes must have been huge. I'd never known someone to hit the jackpot. "The most I ever won was another ticket on those scratch-off games."

"No. Not the actual lottery. I meant it figuratively. I'm the head physical therapist at the Olympic Training Center in town, and I love my job. And believe me, getting paid handsomely to do something you enjoy is like winning the lottery."

I was too embarrassed to delve into the specifics of her job. I couldn't imagine what it was like to meet top-notch athletes in Olympic condition. Henry herself could have passed for an Olympic basketball player. She stood a few inches taller than my five foot seven inches, and her sleeveless polo shirt showcased attractively muscular arms.

"All right, enough bragging. Let me show you your room, and then you can take a nap, watch TV, do whatever." She grabbed my laundry bag, and I followed her downstairs. At the bottom of the stairs, she pointed to two doors on the left. "Laundry room. Bathroom." She walked to the right, and as we passed a bedroom on the left, she pointed. "Spare room." We reached the room at the end of the hall, and she placed the bag on the bed. "Your room. You got cable, HBO, and Showtime. Telephone's here, so call your family. If you don't want to be disturbed, just shut the door, and if I don't see you until it's time to go back, I won't be offended."

"This is like a dream. Thank you so much. Can I help you with anything around the house or in the yard?"

"Nope. If you want company, I'll be upstairs with the football game on, but you don't have to entertain me, and you sure as hell don't have to work for me. There's plenty of food and drink upstairs, no alcohol though. Help yourself, and we'll have supper around six. You like steak?"

"Yes ma'am."

"What?" Henry asked.

"Yes ma'am," I repeated.

"No 'ma'ams,' remember?"

"Yeah." I smiled.

"Good. See ya later." Henry turned, went upstairs, and suddenly the sounds of college football filled the upstairs.

CHAPTER 11

Any initial pangs of jealousy I had for Paige's picture-perfect sponsor family were gone once I saw how cool Henry was and what a kick-ass place she had. I shut the door and put on my issued shorts and T-shirt, then dialed my parent's home and laid back on "my" bed to talk.

I was shocked to find myself crying as soon as I heard their voices. In the past few weeks, I hadn't had time to miss them or be homesick. My contact with them had been one way, just my letters to them. But hearing them now, I realized that I did miss them. They were incredibly proud of what I had accomplished so far, and for the first time, I was proud of me too.

"Have you called Kendra yet?" Mom asked.

"No." And I wasn't planning on it.

"She'll be excited to hear from you! None of your letters made it to her; she was worried." Good old Mom, ever the naïve one. Believing her daughter's former best friend's letters legitimately didn't make it to their destination. And believing her daughter was destined for a life of college, marriage, two-point-five kids, and a minivan.

The rest of the call went predictably. Dad was proud, and Mom was a wreck, wondering when I'd get to call again. She was relieved when I assured her I'd call again before I had to go back that evening. Since we were done with Basic Cadet Training and going into the school year, we'd have phone privileges on the weekends, so I could call more often.

After I hung up the phone, I pulled out my Walkman I had smuggled in and listened to the mixtape I had made during high school. One side was workout-type music with steady, driving beats, and the other side, which I chose to listen to now, was deeper, more reflective music.

The weavings of James Taylor and Melissa Etheridge's slower ballads conjured up memories of home. I reflected on scenes of my childhood and didn't think to be pissed that Kendra was in so many of them. Images of us laughing and having a good time filled my heart with forgiveness and a longing to talk with her and hear her voice.

Lying there on the bed in my new host home in Colorado Springs, having just completed what had been my life's most significant accomplishment, I wanted to share it with Kendra. I had wanted to call her before I called my parents. She would appreciate the adventures, admire the challenges, and tell me how proud she was, and I needed to hear that. I reached over and dialed a number that was more familiar to me than my own home phone number.

"Doll, this better be you." Kendra's psychic phone manners left a lot to be desired. Hearing her voice and knowing that she hadn't changed in the least was a comfort.

"Is that how you answer the phone nowadays?" I asked.

"I knew it was you. Why the hell didn't you write me, bitch? I gotta hear about everything through your mother now?"

"You know why I didn't write." The curse of being friends with Kendra was she knew how to push my buttons and would expect me to forgive her on her time schedule.

"Jesus, Lex, are you still sore about that?" Kendra asked.

"Just drop it, Ken. How are things back at home?"

"Same old, same old. You like it there?"

"Yeah, I really do," I said.

"You kiss any chicks out there, or am I still your only one?"

I slammed the phone down, pissed that I had called Kendra. That was our roller coaster: me wanting to be near her, her pissing me off one way or another, me shunning her, right back to me wanting to be near her. It was this psychotic, dysfunctional relationship, and it drove me absolutely nuts. The normal routine now was to wait for her to call back so she could say something idiotic and hilarious, making us laugh into forgiveness. Not this time. She didn't have the number at Henry's, and I hadn't given it to Mom and Dad either. I wasn't calling Kendra back.

I slid my headphones back on and flipped the Walkman's switch to play the workout side. As the *thumpa thumpa* of bass blared through my head, I closed my eyes and tried to get Kendra out of my head. I couldn't get the volume loud enough to drown out the thoughts of Kendra's assessment of my orientation, so I stopped the tape and went upstairs to watch football with Henry.

CHAPTER 12

"Are you bored already?" Henry asked from the plush sofa square in front of the wide-screen projection television.

"No, just not a big fan of sitting alone."

I grabbed a spot near Henry and watched a blue-and-white team take on a gold-and-black team. We shared a bowl of popcorn and idle chitchat. We both turned our heads to the door when we heard a car pull up in the driveway.

Henry got up and went to the door to see who it was. She made it there just in time to block my view of who it was, but I could hear her as she greeted the visitor, "Hey sweetie, come on in. I didn't think you could be here today. I wasn't expecting you."

Assuming it was Henry's boyfriend, I did a dazed double take when I saw Cadet Teason coming out from behind Henry. She walked in and casually looked over to the couch and said, "Hey, Alexis."

Hearing my first name come from Cadet Teason blew my mind and flipped my stomach even more than the surprise of her presence. I hadn't seen her since the first three weeks of First Beast, after which our upperclass beast masters switched guard.

I guess my face said it all as Henry shot Cadet Teason a disapproving look and said, "You didn't tell her? Terry, go make this right."

Cadet Teason came over to the couch, and just as she sat down, I was already moving to stand up. Apparently, I wasn't required to show respect for upperclassmen like I was required to at the academy because Cadet Teason grabbed me by the waistband and pulled me back down to the couch.

"Here's the deal, Alexis." Hearing my first name from her was foreign. "I switched your sponsor family to Henry. She's my sponsor, too, and I think you'll be more at home here, so when we're here, you're Alexis and I'm Terry. No one back at the Zoo can know about this, understand?"

"Yes ma'am," was all I could say.

Cadet Teason—Terry—shook her head. She patted my thigh with her hand before pushing herself off the couch, using my leg for leverage. "You'll get used to it. The taste of forbidden fruit is worth it."

"Terry, leave us alone," Henry said.

"I'm going. I gotta grab some clothes from my room." Terry disappeared downstairs then reappeared wearing low-rise jeans, a wide black belt, and a snug short-sleeved shirt that highlighted her biceps. She looked amazing, and I felt a desire I knew I shouldn't be feeling for an upperclassman and certainly not for a female upperclassman. Her black dress boots clicked along the tiled foyer as she walked to Henry and kissed her on the cheek. "Bye, Alexis," she said over her shoulder as she left the house.

I swallowed hard as my heart pounded in my throat. My mind was incapacitated by the thought of the brief shower encounter where Terry's breasts had been against my bare skin for a fleeting moment. If that instant in the shower hadn't started my infatuation, hearing my first name from her lips did.

"You okay, kid?" Henry snapped her fingers in front of my face. "Don't worry about Terry. She's a free spirit. I'm sure she's wicked as an upperclassman, but you'll get used to her. Let's watch the rest of the game."

I can't remember the rest of that football game, what Henry served for supper, or the ride back to the academy. Cadet Terry Teason was the only thing on my mind, and I knew that I would never be able to look at her the same way again.

CHAPTER 13

Once the rest of the cadet wing came back to start the academic year, the pressures of being a fourth-class cadet didn't let up any, they just changed. There were now three classes of upperclassmen to harass us, but less time for them to do so. SMACKs served as human alarm clocks and talking CNN tickers. Every morning, we stood out in the hallways shouting that there were ten minutes before the morning meal formation, announcing the uniform of the day, and the breakfast menu. Then we scurried back to our rooms for three minutes, ran back out in the hallways, and shouted the seven-minute mark. During the final five-minute call, the halls were filled with upperclassmen, harassing SMACKs about their three current-event headlines and story summaries. Then the entire cadet wing—four thousand strong— hustled to the Terrazzo, the academy's marble-and-stone checkerboard walking area that hosted our morning and noon meal formations.

Weekends were a welcome reprieve, as most upperclassmen left to be anywhere but the Zoo. The halls were quiet, and freshmen used the silence to catch up on sleep and homework. Attendance at home football games was mandatory, and the first weekend with an away game promised to leave me with more free time than I had had since setting foot on the academy grounds.

Cadet Teason came up to me in the hallway one morning as everyone was heading out to the morning meal formation. She caught me unaccompanied, a massive violation for a SMACK, punishable by loud-volume upper-class yelling. As the lone gazelle trapped by the hungry hyena, I was afraid of the fury that could be unleashed. As an impressionable SMACK preoccupied with the upperclassman in front of me, I was eager for the one-on-one attention. My responsibility as a fourth-class cadet was to stand at a strict position of attention without any emotion.

"Party at Henry's Saturday night. You should come. You can sign out on an overnight pass."

Unsure as to whether this was an order or an invite, I said, "Yes, ma'am." My required military bearing fought against every cell in my body that cheered on the option of grabbing Terry inappropriately.

Cadet Teason smiled. "See you Saturday, Lex."

Not smiling was difficult, but I managed to hold my lips together for one more stoic, "Yes, ma'am."

The rest of the week dragged by, and when Saturday finally arrived, I woke Henry up at seven thirty a.m. with a phone call begging for a ride to her place. I told a few classmates that I was going to be gone Saturday night, and they balked at my blowing an overnight pass so soon in the semester. I played it as just needing to get away since telling my classmates that I was obsessed with Cadet Teason wasn't an option.

"Sorry I woke you," I told Henry as the yellow Mustang peeled away from the academy.

She smiled. "I know it's nice to get away, and I imagine you want to maximize your overnight pass, so it's not a problem."

I was disappointed to learn that Terry wasn't at Henry's house yet and immediately wondered where she was, whom she was with, and what she was doing. Jealous pangs ricocheted against awkward confusion inside me. When Terry showed up later that morning, jealousy and confusion melted me into a naïve, puppy-like follower. I helped clean and organize Henry's place, savoring the shared time with Terry. I felt at home with Terry and Henry as we dusted and scrubbed to loud music. After we had tidied up the house, Henry grabbed three Coors Lights from the fridge and after handing one to Terry, held one out for me.

"I'm not twenty-one," I said.

"Have you ever had a beer?" Henry asked.

I shook my head no.

"Well, as long as you're staying the night, you can drink here. Terry will be your personal drinking buddy to make sure you stay within the limits," Henry said.

I popped the can open, and the chilly scent hit my nose as the beer poured onto my tongue. Based on what I tasted, I couldn't understand the big fascination with beer. I drank it as fast as I could, hoping the beer at the bottom of the can had more flavor than the first few swigs. As I stared at the empty can, I suppressed a fiery belch that brought tears to my eyes. Through those tears I could see Henry and Terry staring back at me with wide eyes while they held their untouched beers.

"Does that mean you're ready for another?" Terry offered me the beer in her hand.

I shrugged my shoulders, stood up from the barstool, and swayed unsteadily as I reached toward Terry's beer.

"Guess again." Henry pulled Terry's arm back. "Why don't you sit out a round?"

I blinked hard to help my eyes focus on Henry and Terry. I was amazed at how quickly the buzz set in, and I realized that maybe this lightheaded relaxation was the flavor of beer that people appreciated.

"Lex, there's something you need to know about tonight," Terry said.

"That's my cue to leave." Henry handed her beer to Terry, gave me a quick peck on the cheek, excused herself, and left the house as she drove off for a date.

"If you see anyone you meet tonight back at the Zoo, you gotta act like you've never seen them before, okay?"

"Why?"

"Look, the people coming over tonight are part of a small community. We don't get much of a chance to meet and socialize anywhere else, so I host the community 'meetings' here." Terry made air quotes as she finished.

The doorbell rang, and she squeezed my shoulder as she walked past. "You'll do fine. We can talk about it later."

I hadn't been much of a partier in high school. I was really more of a hanger-outer, usually just me, Kendra, and Franny. Kendra was always trying to sneak a sip of alcohol from the parental stash of whomever's house we were at, substituting NyQuil if the bar was dry. Franny was flighty enough when sober to fail a sobriety test so there was little advantage to adding alcohol to her system.

As the evening at Henry's wore on, I noticed only women were showing up. Terry was the perfect host.

She set Henry's stereo to play a continual loop of upbeat music that provided a soundtrack to the hum of conversations happening around the room and out on the deck. By the time I had finished my third beer, I was less subtle about watching Terry. I wasn't the only one who couldn't take my eyes off her. She buzzed around the room, and people had one eye on the conversation they were in and one eye looking to see if they were Terry's next stop.

She came by periodically to check on me, thus fulfilling her duties as my drinking buddy. When she mingled in the crowd, I watched her hug and playfully kiss other women on the cheek and felt jealous that she hadn't done that with me.

"You must be the SMACK," a muscular blonde woman said to me, appearing out of nowhere and blocking my view of Terry. "Well, Terry must either be upping her game of pursuit or actually thinking you're pretty special. Usually we only have three degrees and up at the 'meetings.'" She made the same air quotes as Terry had earlier. This woman had the most engaging eyes: blue with specks of yellow-green at the outer edges. I hadn't noticed her eyes when we first met on top of the forty-foot platform on the obstacle course. Her eyes registered no memory of our initial meeting, which was just as well. After my buffoonery up there, I preferred a clean slate with Cadet Cute Blonde.

"So what year are you?" I asked.

"Two degree," she said with what was either an air of superiority or suspicion.

In no time at all, we were in a friendly conversation. Cadet Cute Blonde's actual name was Cameron, but everyone called her Cam. She was from Pennsylvania, but the academy had been her ticket away from a predictable life in the family business, and she really felt she was flourishing here. As we talked, she would frequently touch my arm and was gradually moving closer to me. I tried to back up and give her more space, but the kitchen island we were leaning against prevented me from moving. I slid across the island's front to make more personal space and then her voice lowered in volume. I slid back to hear her, and she grabbed my hand in hers. "Let's go talk out on the deck."

As she pulled me toward the door, I stretched back to the island to grab my beer. Once I had my beer, I started giving way to Cam's pull and looked up in time to see Terry's eyes on us. Terry was in conversation with another girl, but she was clearly focused on Cameron's actions.

Outside on the deck, with the door to the living room closed, it was cooler, peaceful, and much quieter. The view was amazing. Almost a month into fall, the Colorado aspens had started their seasonal shift, decorative swabs of yellow aided city lights dimly illuminating the Rocky Mountain foothills. The academy continued the color palette, its campus easily recognizable by amber lights that dotted the grounds while the seventeen-spired cadet chapel stood tall in its bright-white floodlights. Even from a distance, the academy stood out with pride.

We stood silently against the railing, still holding hands. Cam started moving her fingers against my hand and moved her body closer to mine. This time I didn't move away. I couldn't believe that someone was taking an interest in me, and it felt good to be noticed.

Cam turned toward me. "Isn't this view just breathtakingly romantic?"

The door to the deck opened, and the sounds from the living room interrupted my thoughts before I could answer.

Suddenly, Terry was behind me, wrapping her arms around my stomach, engulfing me in a bear hug. Shivers of excitement went through my body.

Cameron's face went from calm to surprise to anger.

A warm cheek pressed against mine and Terry asked, "Hey kiddo, what are you two up to?"

"Nothing, T, go back inside." Cam's words fought their way through gritted teeth; her voice sounded like a growl.

"Well," explained Terry, "Lex here is my drinking buddy, and I gotta keep an eye on her. Why don't you two come inside?"

"She's okay out here, Terry. I can handle this one. Swing to another vine." Cam's head nodded toward the rest of the party inside while she shot Terry a look that made me feel non-fluent in their secret code.

"Well, I'd feel better if I could see Lex because if she gets too drunk and ends up down there"—Terry pointed to the ground two stories below the deck—"it'll be my ass. C'mon, let's go." Terry spun me around and released one of her arms and put it around Cam and walked the three of us back into the living room.

Once inside, Cameron left my side without saying anything and melted back into the party. I felt as I had just been raffled off and Cameron was the second-highest bidder.

Terry squeezed the arm that was still around my waist, kissed my forehead, and offered me another beer. She never left my side for the rest of the evening. People came and chatted with her, and she introduced me and included me in the conversations.

I caught a glimpse of Cam a few times. She invaded other women's personal space and as the night progressed, she got more and more drunk. By the end of the night, she was sloppily hanging on to the nearest person who was less drunk than her… which was everyone.

But I only cared that I was by Terry's side. Compared to Terry, everyone and everything else seemed to be happening in black and white. Terry was the rainbow in my monochromatic world.

CHAPTER 14

There wasn't much cleaning to do after everyone left. Most of the guests had thrown away their empty bottles and cleaned up after themselves. Terry had made sure that the drunks were paired with sober drivers. She turned the music down, stoked the fire, and sat down next to me on the couch. "Well, sister, did you have fun tonight?"

"Yeah, nice group."

"So what were you and Cam talking about?"

"Nothing really, just about where we're from and stuff. She's nice."

"I think she likes you," Terry said.

"Whatever. It's not like we can hang out back at school. She's a two degree, and I'm scum," I joked.

"Well, do you like her?"

"I guess. I don't know." I wasn't sure where this was really going.

"Have you figured out what the 'community' is?" she asked, again with the air quotes.

"Women in the military." I gave a single shoulder shrug.

"Close." She laughed, and it came out as a nasal snort. "Lex, all the women that were here tonight are gay."

"I'm not," I said with way too much denial to be believed.

Terry continued without acknowledging my denial. "So, you felt nothing out there with Cameron or with me? The goose bumps on your arm when I held you were from the cold? Lex, I saw you watching me. I was watching you too."

I was so confused. I wanted to be straight. Well, not really. I wanted to be straight enough to get through the academy, but I wanted to experience this woman in front of me. I wanted Kendra to be wrong, but I wanted to kiss Terry. Tears welled up in my eyes, and as one escaped down my face, Terry wiped it away with a gentle stroke of her thumb.

"Lexy, it's okay," Terry said quietly.

"No, it's not," I said softly. "How am I going to make it through school if I'm like this?"

"Lexy. We're all like you. How many women were here tonight? Twenty maybe? That's not even everybody. There are a lot of us here at school, and we're all surviving. That's what the community is about. We get together to have an outlet."

"But what about the whole 'incompatible with military service' bullshit?" It was my turn to float the air quotes around the party line for why people like those in the community weren't allowed to serve in the military.

I had so many questions. When did Terry know she was like them? Did she learn from her best friend too? Did she figure it out before she got to the Zoo?

Terry had questions of her own. Her hand cupped my face, waiting to catch more tears. "Have you ever been with a woman?"

"No," I said abruptly.

"Kissed a woman?"

"No." Kendra didn't count in my book.

"I didn't think so." Terry caressed my face. She moved in closer, the fireplace's reflection in her eyes. She closed her eyes, and I felt her lips on mine.

The kiss was gentle and soft, but I wanted more. I opened my mouth wider, inviting her tongue as she kissed me harder. My moans drifted into her mouth, and she echoed them with moans of her own.

We wound up lying side by side on the couch as our kiss continued. I reached up for her chest, something I had wanted to do since that day in the shower, and held her firm tit in my hand.

She untucked her shirt and guided my hand up against her warm skin. She didn't have a bra on, which caught me by surprise. Terry let out a small whimper when I pulled my lips away from hers. I pushed her shirt up to her shoulders, and she pulled it over her head and threw it to the floor. She sighed approvingly when my mouth enveloped her right breast. Her moans of approval increased, and she reciprocated by putting her hand between my legs, squeezing hard to feel through the denim.

She started to push her hand down my jeans, but I stopped her as I unbuttoned and unzipped her pants. "Show me on you."

She held my hand under hers and together we slid into her underwear. She moaned louder as I touched her slick skin. My fingers were coated after a couple strokes and glided easily up and down her. She removed her guiding hand and used it to push her underwear and pants down. She opened up her legs, putting one foot on the floor while the other one slid between my legs and pushed against me. I continued my slow up-and-down pattern until she said, "My clit," and directed my fingers up to a fleshy knob.

She moved my fingers in slow circles, and I realized that in all the sex ed classes I'd had, I'd never learned that little bump could cause a woman as much pleasure as Terry was in right then.

"Oh God, yes," she cried as she left my hand unattended to do what she had taught it. She managed to slide her hand down into my jeans and rubbed my clit through my now-drenched underwear. When she pushed the fabric aside and I felt her fingers, I lost track of what I was doing.

"Don't stop," she panted. I looked down at her naked body as she lay flat on her back and saw my own hand swallowed in between her legs. Her arched back rose and fell with each of my circles and her six-pack abs flexed and shook as I slowly increased my revolutions. Her eyes were closed, and she was breathing faster and faster. She brought her free hand up and tugged at her breasts. I pushed her hand aside with my eager mouth. She literally screamed as I sucked her entire left tit in my mouth. I was afraid I had sucked too hard and was hurting her so I let her go.

"Again. Harder," she cried as she pushed my head back down and thrust her chest back into my mouth. I sucked her back into my mouth and flicked her nipple with my tongue.

"Harder, faster," she said as she thrashed below me. She was grinding against my hand, demanding faster circles.

I tried to keep both fronts stimulated, sucking and releasing her tits while stroking her expanding clit. I could feel her body quiver as I sucked harder and stroked faster. Her hand inside my jeans gripped a handful of my crotch as she arched her back and screamed, "Oh shit, oh shit, oh shit!"

Terry's body convulsed once more with an involuntary shiver and I gently let her tit slide out of my mouth but left my hand on her pussy. Her eyes opened halfway, as if I had just woken her up. A huge grin covered her face and she pulled me down onto her and kissed me. As our kiss continued, I started small soft circles on her clit still beneath my hand. Her head pushed back away from our kiss, her back arched again and her body shivered twice more as I heard her exhale sharply. Her body went limp again and we lay still for a few moments.

"Shit Lex," Terry finally spoke, "There is no way you haven't done that before." She grabbed her shirt from the floor and wiped my hand with it, "I don't think anyone's ever made me that wet. You were amazing." She pulled me down into another kiss, which was interrupted by the phone ringing.

The phone rang once, but Terry didn't get up to get it. The phone went silent for a few moments. It rang again. Silence again. The third time it rang Terry jumped up. "It's Henry, she's on her way back. That's her sign. Help me get dressed," she commanded.

We collected her clothes, and Terry threw them on and ran to the bathroom. I went to the kitchen and grabbed two more beers and met Terry back in the living room. She sat on the chaise lounge and motioned for me to sit with her. I made a disapproving look at the door that Henry was bound to walk through soon. Terry said, "Don't worry about it. Henry will understand. She's one of us."

I didn't need much convincing to be in Terry's arms again. She opened up her legs, and I sat between them and leaned up against her. I could feel her braless chest behind me as she wrapped her arms around me. We sipped our beers and watched the fire.

Henry didn't seem the least bit surprised to see Terry and me cuddled together in front of the fire, although I still couldn't believe it.

"Hey girls." Henry came over to sit on the couch next to us. "How'd it go?"

"Lex had a full night," Terry said. That was an understatement.

"You doing okay, Lex?" Henry asked.

"Yeah, I'm great." Terry squeezed me as I answered. I tried to contain my enthusiasm over the secret connection that Cadet Terry Teason and I now shared.

"You look great," Henry winked. "I, too, had a great evening. I'm officially a proponent of the blind date fix-ups. See you two in the morning." Henry got up from the couch, went into her room, and shut the door.

"Do you wanna stay here or go downstairs," Terry whispered.

"Can we stay here?" I didn't want to move.

"Sure." Terry reached over her head, grabbed a quilt, and threw it over us. I turned sideways, laid my head against her chest, and reached around and held onto her.

"You know neither one of us can talk about this after we leave here, right?" Terry's mouth was right next to my ear, and despite what she was saying I found it a turn-on.

"Lex, you hear me?" Terry asked when I said nothing.

"Mm-hmm," I mumbled.

"I'm glad I was your first," Terry's voice started fading, "But no getting attached."

I thought about her words, but I knew we had something special. She and I had shared a sacred event reserved for married couples on their wedding night. She'd even admitted that no one had touched her like I had. The class difference would make interactions at school very limited, but we had a safe haven here at Henry's.

I stayed awake, feeling her legs against mine. As I tucked the covers under my chin, I smelled Terry's musky scent still on my fingers. Being with her made me feel safe and, better yet, made me feel normal. I let myself enjoy her lingering smell as her rhythmic breathing put me to sleep in her arms.

CHAPTER 15

After my induction into the community, it was hard to focus on the real reason I was in Colorado Springs. Classes were tough, and everyone carried a full academic load of twenty-one semester hours. It was nice that there was no class distinction in that regard. We were all suffering under the academic pressures.

Military requirements added to the degree of difficulty in a SMACK's life. Each day, if requested, doolies were expected to spout off the menus for all three meals, summarize three current event articles, pop off a quote verbatim from any page of *Contrails*, as well as know every upperclassman's full name and hometown. Memorizing data came easy for me, but it was the element of surprise that always got me. We would be in the middle of a training session, which was really just a bunch of upperclassmen yelling at a line of SMACKs in the hallway, and without warning, an upperclassman would ask you to recite the third verse of "The Star-Spangled Banner," which would be a hell of a lot easier if they'd let you sing it. Then without transition, ask you what the breakfast menu had been that day. I actually enjoyed yelling out in the hall. I was good at it, and as a result, upperclassmen usually left me alone. It was a nice release from a day of sitting in classrooms. On days when I had too much homework and too little time, training sessions gave me an approved opportunity to scream at the top of my lungs.

My life ran parallel with Terry's since we were in the same squadron and shared the same sponsor. Each day provided numerous occasions to see her. Even though I was the SMACK against the wall and she was the upperclassman pacing in front, waiting for someone to screw up, it was exciting to see her. It was hard for me to hide my overpowering feelings for her, and one day I absentmindedly smiled at her.

"Eerie Cat, what are you smiling about?" demanded a male voice from my left.

"Sir, I do not know."

"Is this funny to you?" barked a familiar voice, now from the right.

"I think we got us a funny girl here," said Cadet Terry Teason, now standing right in front of me.

"No ma'am," I yelled.

"Well, then Eerie Cat, would you like to tell us all what you're smiling about?" Cadet Teason asked.

This made me smile even bigger, and the smile made it hard to say, "No ma'am," without laughing. I'm not sure if Terry figured it out, but she let up and handed the primary scolding off to one of her classmates. "I don't know what to do with this one. Cadet Fuentes, she's yours."

Cadet Fuentes stepped up and through his thick Latin accent let me know that my antics, though valiant, were not going to take the pressure off of my classmate who didn't know his quotes. Apparently, in my daydream state, I had taken the heat off of Pipes, who could not recite the "Purpose of the Fourth-Class System" verbatim from *Contrails*.

Pipes had been recruited to play football at the academy, and being the moneymaker that the football team was, football players tended to skate by on the minimums. Pipes appreciated my effort and came into our room to thank me after we'd been excused from the hallway.

"Why are you so sweet to me?" he asked.

"It wasn't intentional, but I'm glad it helped."

"You know I can take it, don't you? I don't need you getting your assed chewed to save mine."

"Then it won't happen again," I said.

"You know." He moved closer to me. "Some of the team is getting together for a party this weekend.

You wanna be my date?" Pipes dragged his fingers clumsily up my arm as he whispered his question against my neck.

I jumped from his touch, but I wasn't sure why. "I don't have many passes left, Pipes, but thanks for the offer." As four degrees, we were only allowed three day passes and two overnight passes. I'd already blown one overnight pass at Henry's and wanted to save the other one in case another opportunity with Terry arose.

"Okay, but a fine gal like you won't go dateless forever. Keep me in mind," Pipes proposed, then left my room.

Paige, with her perfect timing, walked in as Pipes was leaving. "Well, what were you and Pipes up to? What'd I miss?" Paige asked.

"Nothing."

"Why not? He's hot."

"Well, then you go for him. I'm trying to keep my head above water with school and getting yelled at all the time."

"I could do a fling with him, but nothing long term. He just seems like he'd be a good fuck."

"Paige!" I had never heard her use a foul word before, and hearing the mother of all bad words in such a context shocked me.

"What? Haven't you ever just used a guy for sex?"

"No."

"Well, it's great. You get off, he gets off, and you go about your day. My best friend back home and I have that arrangement. FTF, that's what we call it, friends that fuck."

"I'm seeing a whole new side of you, Paige, but I think that's quite enough for one night. I'm going to the showers." I shook Paige's revelation from my head, put on my robe, and grabbed my towel. I'd learned that showering at night was less crowded and less rushed, so I could take my time.

"Lex, you've been with a guy, right?" Paige grabbed my robe to pull me back into a conversation I didn't want to be in.

"As opposed to what?" As soon as I said it, I wished I hadn't.

"As opposed to a woman."

That was exactly where I had inadvertently steered the conversation and precisely the destination I didn't want to arrive at.

"Holy shit, Paige! I wouldn't be here at a military school if I'd been with a chick! And of course I've been with a guy," I lied.

Panic prevented any witty words to get me out of the corner in which I'd put myself. The best reply I could come up with was a 180-degree spin and an immediate departure from the room. I was in damage control mode, but as I sped toward the showers, I wondered if I'd just done more damage by my defensive retort and quick departure.

As I showered in solitude, I thought about Paige's FTF concept and Pipes's proposition. If I tried sex with a guy, at least I could figure out if that's what I was missing while also donning the costume of a flaming heterosexual to throw off people like Paige. Or maybe I could have sex with men but relationships with women. That'd be okay, wouldn't it? I figured as long as I had sex with a man, I couldn't be accused of being gay. I toweled off and stood in front of the long mirror, running a comb through my short hair when the door opened.

"Good evening, Cadet Teason," I said quietly as I came to attention.

Terry peeked under the bathroom stalls to make sure that we were the only ones in there. She stood behind me and smiled at me in the mirror. Being the sole recipient of her smile erased Paige, Pipes, and heterosexuality from my mind.

"You coming to Henry's anytime soon?" she asked.

"Not sure."

"You should. I'd like to see you again."

"You see me every day," I said, realizing what she'd meant as soon as I said it.

Terry stepped closer and put her hands on my hips, sliding one hand into the gap in my robe. Her touch took the breath out of me as she whispered, "Henry's going out of town this weekend. Can I pick you up early Saturday morning?"

I swallowed hard as I nodded my head. I put my hand over hers when she tried to move it away. "Please," I said.

"Not here. I'll pick you up Saturday, down at the gym. Is six thirty too early?" Terry asked.

"No."

"See you then. I can't wait." Terry kissed my ear as she pulled her hand out from under my robe. I closed my eyes and felt unsteady. Terry held me up as I wobbled. She smiled at me again in the mirror, winked, then left. I saw my red face in the mirror, could hear my heart pounding a thousand beats a minute, and could still feel Terry's touch. I splashed cool water on my face, composed myself, then headed back to my room.

CHAPTER 16

I could barely sleep Friday night, and by the time my alarm went off at six a.m., I was already awake. I took a quick shower, made sure my bits and pieces were clean shaven, threw on my PT gear, and jogged down to the gym. Henry's car was waiting by the time I got there at six twenty, and I thought there had been a change of plans.

I jumped in and was relieved to see Terry at the wheel. "Henry spent the night with her girlfriend. We got the Mustang," she said as we sped off toward Henry's place.

"What'd you do last night?" I didn't really care about the answer since it probably wouldn't change the course of today.

"Why?" She put her hand on my leg. "Did you miss me?"

"I couldn't sleep last night. I almost called you to come get me last night. Of course, I only have one more overnight pass left for the semester, so I'll have to save that for something special."

"Oh, I see, I'm not special enough to blow an overnight on, eh?" Terry laughed.

I opened my mouth to try and explain my foot out of my mouth but let the awkward moment pass as we drove on.

We pulled into Henry's garage, and before the garage door had closed behind the car, Terry reached over and kissed me like she had missed me. I felt like I was sitting on a powerful secret. And I was. I was being kissed by the same disciplinarian who yelled at me and my classmates. I was empowered by the thrill of the unauthorized relationship.

I pulled away from her kiss slightly, using a sliver of space between our lips as the lure to bring her closer to me. She leaned into the kiss, and I lured her once again to my side of the car. The seat belt chaperone restrained any further pursuit, and Terry let the seat belt reel her back to her side of the car, breaking our kiss. She unbuckled herself and rather than continue our kiss, she opened the car door and stepped out into the garage.

I followed her into Henry's house, where the smell of vanilla candles accompanied warm, amber light as the sun finished its rise. The kitchen table was set for two with a small circle of pillar candles still burning.

When I came back upstairs after changing into jeans and a T-shirt, she held my chair out for me as I sat down to a plate of breakfast burritos. We ate then cleaned up and sat on the couch. Simply sitting there with Terry brought back the sounds of the fire, the scent of her, the image of her arched back and intense orgasm from our first night together. Was seven a.m., right after breakfast, too early to attack someone? I figured it was.

"Have you ever had sex with a boy?" Then I wondered why I had asked and whether I really wanted to know her answer. I was fine living in my fantasy world that I was her first and only.

"No, why?"

"Just something my roommate and I were talking about." I suddenly wished I hadn't brought it up.

"Do we have to talk about this today?"

"No," I said quickly, thankful she was ending the mess I started. "So what is the plan for today?"

She pulled me toward her and the momentum brought us horizontal. I let her continue her controlled fall as I slid a pillow under her head, straddled her stomach, and kissed her.

"This is what I had in mind for today," Terry said in between kisses. Terry wasn't big on talking anyway. Her body language was louder than any conversation I wanted at that moment.

We kissed on the couch until kissing wasn't enough, and I wanted to feel her and pleasure her. I unsnapped a few snaps on the side of her Adidas warm-ups, put my hand in, and rubbed her through her underwear. They were silk and lacy and the thought of something so petite and ladylike under those tomboy sweats made me undo the rest of the snaps in one quick rip.

"Shit," was all I could get out. A small patch of hot pink fabric made a tiny upside down triangle over a thin patch of brown hair. I ran both hands over her midsection and around her backside to reveal more about her underwear. It was a lacy silk, G-string thong. Except for a few Victoria's Secret catalogs, I'd never seen anything like this. I was surprised how erotic and horny it made me feel. I bent down to kiss the triangle and could smell her strong scent. I'd never kissed anyone below the belt, but that wasn't stopping my desire to lick her.

Terry blocked my kiss by rolling over, leaving me to look at her perfect bare ass. I touched it lightly, afraid that making full contact would wake me out of this fantasy. Terry got up with a swift push-up, pulled me up, and led me downstairs to her bedroom. She pulled her shirt over her head and stood in a pink silk lace bra that matched her panties and took my breath away.

"There's something I've been dying to do," Terry said, undoing the button and fly on my jeans then peeling them down to the floor. She pushed me back onto the high bed and I shimmied back from the edge until Terry grabbed my legs behind my knees and pulled me forward. She leaned over from her standing position and kissed me on the lips. She pulled my shirt up, slowly kissed my stomach, then my belly button and then her hands and mouth continued their journey south.

When she kissed me through my underwear, the heat from her mouth and the pressure of her moist tongue made me forget everything. She slowly and gently pulled my underwear from my hips, kissing my skin as she exposed it. As her hands pulled my underwear over my thighs, calves, and feet, her mouth stayed on my pussy. She licked me from the bottom up and the contrasting sensations of the room's cool air and her hot tongue spiked my entire body with a prickly sensation. After endless up-and-down passes with her tongue, she focused on the top of my mound and her head moved in circles, carrying her tongue in the same pattern.

The soft touch of her finger barely reaching into me below her tongue brought me into my own back-arching earthquake of involuntary muscle contractions. My groin was throbbing and I was breathing so hard and fast that hyperventilation was sure to follow. Suddenly, I shuddered and came with intense spasms that seemed to have no end.

She didn't move and I couldn't. I lay there motionless and exhausted as she crawled up next to me. "Was that okay?"

"Lex?" she tried to get my attention again, "Are you okay?"

"I never knew that's what it felt like."

"What? An orgasm?"

That word embarrassed me, but the truth embarrassed me more. "No, sex."

"Are you still playing that, 'This is my first time' gig?" Terry asked.

"I can no longer say that truthfully," I said.

Terry just laughed. "I haven't taken a shower yet, why don't you come in with me? I know you've showered with a woman before." She winked.

"You knew that was me?" I was reaching new levels of embarrassment.

"I would have spoken up sooner if it were anyone else."

"Why'd you say anything at all?"

"Because my classmates were there too. Staying in there with you would have been a little on the obvious side. So how about it?"

Terry had a way of making me feel like complete putty, molding me into whomever she wanted me to be. I loved being around her, and I loved being with her. If she wanted to share a shower, I wasn't going to refuse.

"As long as we get more than fifteen seconds," I joked.

The shower stall was roomy with shampoo and conditioner bottles that sat on a large corner seat. Terry removed my bra, unclasped hers, and shed her panties without ever taking her eyes off of me. She reached over my shoulder to feel the water's temperature and walked in behind me. The short hair from her crotch tickled my butt and her hard nipples pressed against my back. The water cascaded over us and we may as well have been under an exotic waterfall.

She grabbed a bar of soap and lathered my back, rubbing her chest against the foam. She ran her soapy hand between my legs and triggered jolts of pleasure left over from her recent feast. Keeping her hand in place, she turned me so my back was against the shower's wall and used her knee to nudge my leg into a bent position, placing my foot on the corner seat. Terry pressed her body against mine, straddling my straight leg with hers, still rubbing back and forth with her hand. I reached in between her legs and reached beyond her clit, dragging her slick lubricant onto my fingers and back to her clit. Her indecipherable words let me know this was more than okay.

Her fingers went farther between my legs and I felt her penetrate me. She moved slowly in and out, gently but deeply. Having her inside me made me feel so connected to her and made it hard to focus on pleasuring her. She continued with a few more patient strokes, pulled out, then entered with painful pressure. I winced and grabbed at my crotch, now burning with pain.

Terry pulled herself out of me and sounded concerned, "Oh God, Lex, I'm so sorry." At the same time, we looked down and saw the shower water rinsing off her three bloody fingers. Red water disappeared down the drain, taking my official virginity with it.

"Lex, I'm so sorry. I honestly thought," she cut herself short. "I'm sorry." She held me and helped me wash the remaining blood from my broken hymen. She was tender and apologetic. I was again embarrassed, but thankful that of all the people I could have had this moment with, it was with Terry.

Later, we went back up to the living room, where we lounged on the couch, ate popcorn, and watched movies on HBO. We fell asleep on each other and after about forty-five minutes, I snapped awake, afraid that I had slept past my day pass's curfew. I wouldn't be in serious trouble if I didn't make it back by nine o'clock, but it was the kind of attention a SMACK didn't need or want.

I looked at the clock and was calmed to see that it wasn't even noon yet. Terry was still snoozing, laid back in the corner section of the couch, legs spread eagle. I couldn't resist. I put my hand down her pants to find my way unhindered by any underwear. I began to unbutton her shirt with my other hand and made a trail of kisses down her bare stomach as she had on mine. Terry moved slightly but didn't wake up until I had knelt on the floor and pushed her pants down to her ankles. She kicked them off and smiled down at me.

I was staring right into Terry's cave as it shined with its wetness. I wanted to kiss and lick Terry's pussy, assuming it would make me feel as good as when she had gone down on me. Still, I was afraid of how it would taste, whether I would gag or whether I'd be any good.

She put her hand on my head and pushed me in closer. The smell gave me confidence. I wanted to be with her, wanted her in my mouth, wanted to taste her. I dived in. Softly at first, but not for long. I licked her, trying to mimic how she had tasted me. Primarily, I listened to her responses to see what she liked. I had read an article in *Men's Health* magazine about how a man should please his woman, it suggested drawing the alphabet with your tongue. I gave this a try and by "H" Terry was grinding her hips and grabbing handfuls of my hair, which I took to be a good sign. By "W" my tongue was tired, but Terry was still enjoying my tongue's penmanship.

I started to rub her with my fingers and before long she begged, "Go in me."

Now that I was inside, I didn't know what to do. Whatever she had done to me had hurt and caused bloodshed and I didn't want to mimic that. *Men's Health* hadn't covered this particular subject, probably because men used a completely different "finger." So there I was, between her legs, finger inside her, without a clue. Using the same technique I had with my tongue, I just started making large, slow circles inside her, looking for a spot that made her moan.

Slowly. Slowly. Nothing.

Slowly. Slowly. Nothing. Shit.

I resumed gentle licks and tried the alphabet in cursive. Soft moan. Thank God for my tongue because the circles inside her weren't working. I needed to hit more spots inside her. Maybe in and out along with the circles. Slowly in, around, out, around, in, around. The moan. Yes. It was the in and out that she liked.

"More," Terry cried.

More what? Did that mean lick faster? Did she mean move faster? Could she possibly mean use more fingers? In a split second I decided fingers made the most sense. I pulled my finger out and pushed two back in.

"Oh, yes," she said, "in and out."

Mesmerized, I watched my fingers appear and disappear inside Terry. Her cries got louder and her body began to tremble the way it had before.

"Oh God. More!" I thrust a third finger inside.

"Eat me!" she screamed. I tore myself away from the thrill of watching my fingers fuck her and laid my tongue onto her clit. Her hips brought her pussy up into my mouth and I fucked her faster and sucked her harder. "Oh God, Erecat!" she shouted.

I paused briefly at hearing my name hollered as if we were in the halls of the academy and I was fucking up my recitation of the day's current events. Then I realized not what I was fucking but whom I was fucking. I was the one in control. I was the one orchestrating the moment.

Cadet Teason's impending orgasm renewed the energy in my cramping hand and crippled tongue. Four more quick circles on her clit and three more in and outs and I felt her pussy clamp down on my fingers, holding them in as her orgasm rippled through her body.

Her juices dribbled down my arm, making me smile as I remembered that no one made her as wet as I did. Tenderly, I wiped her legs and my face off, noticing that we'd need to wipe down the couch before Henry got home. Terry motioned me up with open arms. I straddled her unmoving body and hugged her while she caught her breath.

"You are amazing," she finally said.

"I love being with you. I don't want to go back tonight."

Terry's face changed with the reminder that my curfew was approaching. We still had eight hours, but the thought of being alone in my crowded room back at the academy when I could be here with Terry put a pit in my stomach.

"If you stayed here another night, will you be ignoring homework that needs to be done?" Terry asked.

"What do you think I did all Friday night when I couldn't sleep? Would I be cramping your plans if I stayed here one more night?"

Terry's face got a mischievous grin. "No, but this will be your last overnight pass for the semester. Nothing would make me happier than if you were to call and turn your day pass into an overnight."

I'd have to call the CCQ, or Cadet in Charge of Quarters, who is basically a secretary for the entire squadron. Three degrees had this shit duty, since SMACKs couldn't be trusted and two degrees and firsties were above such tasks.

One quick call later, I had converted my day pass into my last overnight pass. The pit in my stomach was gone and I had the whole afternoon, evening, night, and next day with Terry. Terry grabbed the cordless from me and dialed as she finished her call downstairs. I waited on the couch and questioned her on her phone call when she returned.

"No one, just something I had to cancel," she said.

"Another date?"

"Something like that. Let's watch another movie." She answered with a tone that didn't match what I had posed as a joke, but I let it go. Well, I tried to let it go, but it nagged at me from the back of my mind. Paige's FTF concept engulfed my thoughts, and I wondered if I was Terry's FTF and if I should get an FTF of my own.

CHAPTER 17

Terry and I relaxed the rest of the afternoon, and as we thought about supper she remembered that Henry, and possibly her date, were headed home that night.

"Shit, we better call and let her know we're still here in case they had plans of their own." Terry winked. She called Henry at her girlfriend's house, and when she told her we were in the house for another night you could hear Henry's excited voice through the receiver. A short planning session ensued, which, based on Terry's questions and replies, raised some challenges.

Terry seemed charged up when she got off the phone. "We're going out to a club tonight."

"You are or we are?" I tried to clarify since public appearances at a club were complicated by the facts that I was under twenty-one and a SMACK. Fourth-class cadets at the academy weren't allowed to wear civilian clothes until they were three degrees. Many of my classmates tried to get away with it, but only in places farther from the academy, like Denver, an hour's drive away. So unless we were driving a good distance away, I didn't know how we were going to pull this off.

Terry produced her driver's license from her wallet. It was a Pennsylvania license with the text "Valid without photo pending licensee's return" in the square where a photo normally went.

"You have until tonight to memorize everything on this ID because tonight, you are Theresa Teason, got it?" Terry said.

"What if someone sees me?" I asked.

Terry came over and hugged me. "Lex, we're going to a gay bar. If anyone from the Zoo sees us there, they'll have the same concern of being seen there." This took a while to process, but once I got over that, I had to digest the fact that gay people had their own bar.

Henry and Josie, her girlfriend of five weeks, came back to the house bearing grocery bags. They sent us out to Josie's Jeep to get the rest of the bags. The four of us worked together in the kitchen and out at the grill to make a filling dinner of steak, salad, baked potatoes, French bread, and Sara Lee cheesecake. Henry's kitchen was normally roomy, but with four people milling about, there was a lot of physical contact with sly hands running along backsides. We sat and ate supper like a family of four then retired to the living room couch with an after-dinner beer.

"What did you two lovebirds do last night?" Terry asked Henry and Josie.

"We had a wonderful night at the Broadmoor and played a complete round of golf before brunch this morning," Josie said. The Broadmoor was a classy resort where it wasn't cheap to stay, golf, or eat, so for them to have done all three was a high-ticket affair.

"I know Terry wasn't even up by the time we were at the eighteenth hole," Henry said.

"You must golf pretty early. I was here eating breakfast by six forty-five," I said.

Terry shifted from her perch on the couch's armrest as I playfully elbowed her.

Henry's face contorted with confusion. "Ah. A little early for the breakfast plan, isn't it, Terry?" I was a little confused, but Terry said nothing, and Henry didn't give her a chance. "And Lex, did you get another overnight pass or is this your second and final one for the semester?"

"What's with the interrogation?" Josie asked.

"Mmmm, nothing." Henry nodded her head as if she had just discovered something important.

"How long have you two been together?" Josie asked in our general direction.

Just as Terry said, "Oh, we're not together," I said, "Five weeks."

As soon as I'd registered what Terry's answer had been, I felt like a fool. In all the demeaning situations I had been in as a basic cadet and a SMACK, none compared to how humiliated I felt during the silence that followed.

"We're still going out, so everyone freshen up. The Jeep leaves in thirty minutes. Lexy, you help me clean off the table." Henry filled both hands with dishes from the table as she carried them to the kitchen sink.

"I'll help too," Terry said.

"No, you go get ready." Henry pointed her chin toward the stairs and shot Terry a narrowed-eye glance.

I brought the rest of the dishes to Henry at the sink. "You okay, kiddo?" Her raspy voice was tender and almost at a whisper.

"Yeah, dinner was great, and I haven't had a steak in forever."

"I'm not talking about supper." Henry paused, took a deep breath in then out. "Terry's great. She's fun, smart, and outgoing. Everyone's attracted to her, and she plays on that. That's what makes her a heartbreaker, and she's left a heap of broken hearts in this town. I will say she's been different with you. You're the first fourth-class cadet in the community, but she's still a heartbreaker at her core. Maybe Terry needs a sip of her own medicine, and you, my dear, may be the first person in a position to do it."

I had no clue what to say next, so I blurted out, "I've never been to a bar before."

Henry just laughed, winked, grabbed my shoulders, and kissed me. It was a thoughtful, mysterious kiss. It was more than a peck, but less than making out. Our mouths were open but without total contact. She was sensitive, perceptive, attentive, and caring, and I will never be able to explain how it was the most perfect kiss I ever had.

CHAPTER 18

I regained my composure and looked forward to this next adventure in my life, which would fulfill a lot of unresolved "bad girl" things I had never done. I wasn't just going to a bar, I was going to a gay bar. I wasn't just going to a gay bar, I was unlawfully using someone else's ID to get in. Add on the fact that I was a SMACK illegally in civilian clothes, fraternizing with an upperclassman of the same sex, in the same squadron, and drinking underage. The Air Force Academy Security Police would need a second page to list my numerous infractions on the rap sheet.

I smiled with false confidence, bounded down the stairs, and jumped into the open doorway of Terry's room. "Come on, slow poke, let's go."

Terry sat on the edge of the bed as if she were waiting for me. Her elbows were planted on her knees as she leaned forward in a stooped slouch like a benched basketball player. "Lex, come here, I owe

"

you an explanation." Terry patted the bed, motioning for me to sit next to her.

"No time, Jeep's leaving."

"Are you okay?" she asked.

"Yeah." I tackled her on the bed and lay on top of her. I gave her a kiss like I'd seen her give other women at the party. "We're just having fun, let's go."

Terry didn't seem totally convinced, but seeing her unsure of herself for the first time gave me an intoxicating feeling of control and confidence. By the time I dragged her by the hand upstairs, she was in a better mood. I hugged her in the back of the Jeep while I made mental notes of the roads since I knew I'd be driving us home.

The navigation would be an easy one as we went south on I-25 and turned onto West Colorado Avenue to the Hide and Seek complex. I lost some of my confidence as I held Terry's Pennsylvania license in my sweaty hand. Henry and I went in first, leaving Josie and Terry a few minutes behind in case the bouncer recognized Terry's name on two separate IDs. He never balked at my pictureless ID, and we walked past him into the booming bass of the club. Henry grabbed my hand and pulled me out onto the dance floor.

The floor was so packed with bodies that everyone was forced into a common choreography.

Henry led us right into the sea of dancers, faced me, grabbed my back and pulled me close to her. I threw my arms around her neck and let my body melt into hers. It wasn't too long before Josie and Terry split us up and I was grinding hips with Terry. We danced until our shirts were sweaty. I rested my head on Terry's shoulder, feeling safe and special in her arms. Then I thought about Terry's revelation about our relationship, or lack thereof. I was warned about the "microwave friendships" that took place at the academy as people from unconnected backgrounds were thrown into situations with similar troubles, where instant bonds were created out of necessity, proving the misery-loves-company theory. Five weeks was a rapid rate at which to develop a relationship, especially with our circumstances. It dawned on me that Terry had been the only girl I had been with, and I didn't want to miss out on other opportunities by limiting myself to someone who thought little more of me than a fling.

"I think that chick is checking you out." My eyes shot straight toward a beautiful woman who wasn't checking Terry out.

Terry peered over her shoulder. "She's hot."

"Why don't you show me your moves?" I pushed her toward the bar where the blonde sat.

"I wouldn't want to make you jealous."

"Jealous of your moves?" I asked.

"No. Jealous when I'm dirty dancin' with blondie."

I shot her a sly grin. "Tell you what, first one back out on the dance floor with another partner wins." I didn't wait for Terry to agree to the terms as I headed farther down the bar toward a woman who was either interested in the back of Terry's head or me. We had smiled back and forth with locked eyes while I had danced with Terry, and although not unattractive, she was more in my league than blondie.

As I neared the chick at the bar, I began to question the way I had read her signs as she turned back to face the bar. Too proud to admit defeat, I racked my brain for the worst pickup line I could come up with. If Terry was going to beat me at this game, at least I would have fun in the process.

"Excuse me, I just started writing a phone book, can I have your number?" I hoped she would take me seriously enough to engage in a conversation but realize the cheesiness of my line was my attempt to humor her.

"Seriously? That's the best you can do?" She smiled with her hands on her hips, confirming I had succeeded in humoring her.

"Let me try again." I dug deep for more bad lines. "I'm new in town, can I get directions to your apartment?"

She laughed, and I loved being responsible for that, to the point that I almost forgot the competition I was in with Terry. To expedite getting her on the dance floor, I grabbed her ass with one hand and issued my final bad pickup line. "Is this seat taken?"

She liked that line the best, and the music's volume forced her to move her mouth close to my ear so she could introduce herself. I'll be damned if I could remember her name. It wasn't important to me. Getting what's-her-name on the dance floor was.

With my hand still firmly on her backside, albeit a little higher, I led her on the dance floor. I was shocked by my own boldness in my interaction with this woman but knew most of the courage came from the competition. I walked past Terry's back as she made hopeless advances at blondie.

Henry and Josie missed none of it and smiled as they watched me walk onto the dance floor with what's-her-name. Henry leaned back against the bar, tapped Terry on the back, and pointed to the dance floor's newest couple.

Terry's face and body deflated as she realized her defeat.

It felt good to dance with this stranger, but I wasn't sure why. She wasn't a great dancer, and I didn't know anything about her. All signs pointed to one of two reasons for my happiness: winning a trivial contest against Terry or making her look the way she made me feel earlier in the evening.

CHAPTER 19

What's-her-name and I danced until her friends arrived, and she dragged me to meet them. After a rapid round of introductions, all but one headed for the dance floor. That left me with the familiar face of Cameron, the girl from the community's first gathering of the school year.

"Small world." I smiled, remembering Terry's apparent disapproval of Cameron and me together. We stood too close as we talked about nothing in particular. The excitement I had felt when I first met Cam was replaced by the excitement of pissing Terry off if she saw us together.

It didn't take long before Terry came over. "Hey kiddo, we're leaving." Terry gave a slight nod in Cam's direction.

"I can drive her home, Terry." Cam pulled me back toward her.

"Nice try, but Lex is our driver."

"What is it with you two?" I shook my head.

"Well, the Jeep's leaving, we gotta go." Terry left my question unanswered and pulled me away to the parking lot.

As I drove, Henry and Josie were doing some heavy petting in the back seat, probably trying to get what they could for fear of passing out by the time they got home. But they were still conscious and pawing each other when we got back to the house.

Henry and Josie were going to be the only ones having sex back at the house despite Terry's best efforts to get me to spend the night in her room and bed. I lied about being tired, shut the door to my room, and crawled into bed. I couldn't sleep because I couldn't get Terry's denial of us out of my head. As attracted as I was to Terry, I didn't want to fool around with someone who didn't acknowledge it as a relationship. Now I wasn't sure I even wanted a relationship. The community get-together had shown me that there were plenty of women like me right there at school. The bar had been filled with women just like me, and that was only my first time there. I was overwhelmed and confused.

CHAPTER 20

Usually Kendra was my stalwart rock when I was overwhelmed and confused. She had an enviable lackadaisical approach to any sort of dilemma. Even life's catch-22s were simple decisions to her, and she could usually convince me out of gray into black or white.

"Hey, Ken." I spoke quietly into the phone when Kendra picked up on the other end.

"Hey, doll, what's wrong?"

"Can't I call my supposed best friend and just chat?"

"Well, normally I'd say yes, but seeing as how the last time we talked you got all pissed off and hung up on me, I'd say that now something's up." Kendra spoke with such certainty that on any other day I would fight her merely on principle. Tonight, I was too tired.

"Ken, I just need to talk, all right?"

"What's up?"

I didn't know where to start. On the other end of the phone was the person who had always been my sounding board, but I couldn't commit to bouncing off all of the thoughts in my head on Kendra. I settled with, "It's complicated."

Kendra's silence prompted me to say, "Kendra, are you there?"

"Just waiting, doll." And she did, because she knew that eventually I would unload my thoughts into the silence she provided.

I juggled pronouns in my head and gave her a straight version of the situation I was in. "There's a guy here who seems interested in me."

"That's great, Lex! Go for it!"

"It's not that easy, Ken. He's an upperclassman, and even if he admitted we were in a relationship, we can't be seen together, and everything is always so secretive." I had to speak slower than normal for fear of saying "she" instead of "he."

"I would think the sneaking around would add a level of excitement."

"It doesn't, Ken. If I'm going to risk staying at the academy by being with him, then I'd like to think the risk is worth it. As it is, he doesn't even acknowledge our relationship to the only two people who know we're fucking around."

"Then don't waste your time, doll. See what other options there are. You haven't been there long enough to sample the other relationship prospects. If this person really wants to be with you, then they won't stand for you being with anyone else. You control you, no one else. Remember that. If what you're doin' isn't making you happy, keep searching until you find what does."

I appreciated Kendra's genderless references and at this point didn't care whether she thought I was talking about a man or a woman. Still, I wasn't going to let her in on the true identity of my first sexual experience. So many indicators pointed at "gay," but the shock of the fact that my only sexual experience had been with a woman rocked any conviction that I was.

"Lex, are you sure you even need to be with someone right now? Don't you have enough on your plate with the academy?"

"It's not that bad." She did have a point though. Maybe I was just a glutton for punishment.

Kendra's reasoning fit my character better. "Leave it up to you to challenge yourself a little extra. Going to the academy isn't enough. Excelling at the academy, which I'm sure you're doing, isn't enough. You gotta go and step it up a bit by messing around with an outlawed upperclassman." She had me softly laughing by the end of her short sermon.

And then in typical Kendra fashion, she caused the cessation of the laughter she had just created. "Gee, Lex, I guess the only way to make it any more complicated would be if the upperclassman was an upperclasswoman."

The "fuck off" I wanted to say to Kendra couldn't get to my lips because both of us knew she was right.

Kendra read the silence as if she was right next to me on the bed, not seventeen hundred miles away. When a tear started sliding down my face, Kendra sensed it and wiped it away with her rare gentle and caring voice. "Lex, it's okay. I know you think it's not, but it is. Stop fighting it and figure out how you can do this. I know you want to be there and make it through, so you're gonna have to figure out how to balance your wants and the school's requirements. You got it?"

"Yeah." It was like listening to the coach as he picked you up off the ground, dusted you off, and gave you that nudge toward the goal. To Kendra, it was as simple as be gay *and* go to the academy, no sweat.

"And Lex," she was still talking.

"Yeah?"

"If this chick ain't treating you right, she doesn't deserve you. Don't be tempted by the forbidden fruit. Find somebody who really cares about you."

She threw out the advice not only because she'd been waiting to say it, but also because she truly meant it.

I began to wonder how I could be sure I was gay, even though Kendra was adamantly sure I was gay. I wondered if having sex with a man would change me from being attracted to women. Maybe I felt the way I did because women were more familiar to me. I felt compelled to at least give sex with a man a shot, and there was only one guy I trusted and liked enough to try it with.

CHAPTER 21

"Pipes, are you spending Thanksgiving with your girlfriend?" I asked, knowing he and his girlfriend had called it quits before he left for the academy. He was born and raised in Colorado Springs, so he had a home-cooked Thanksgiving meal waiting and ready for him.

"Nope, the team is having Thanksgiving together at my parents' house. I was thinking about blowin' outta here Wednesday night and hangin' at a hotel. You wanna come with me?" His proposition and word choice dripped with sexual innuendos, and he looked shocked when I told him I was very interested.

"Maybe I can see why they really call you 'Pipes,' Pipes," I laid it on as I traced my finger from his shoulder down the middle of his chest. "What time are you gonna pick me up?"

"Honey, I don't think you can handle what I got to offer." He winked.

My tone switched from jovial jest to nervous truth in jest. "You may be right, Pipes, but maybe you can do me as a favor."

"You mean, do you a favor?"

"No. I mean do me as a favor."

Clearly, he was confused. I had to explain my inexperience and my desire to give it a go with someone I trusted. Disbelief replaced his confusion, and then gratitude replaced his disbelief.

"Thanks for trusting me that much, Lex," Pipes said.

I didn't have the heart to tell him I didn't trust him enough with the deeper revelation about my sexual experience.

"Well, I've only been with my ex-girlfriend, so I don't want you to get your hopes up."

"Why's that? Won't your hope be up?" I changed the mood as I let my finger trail a little closer toward his "hope." Hanging out with Kendra and Franny had warped me enough to allow me to pretend that I had experience.

We went over some of the mechanics of this possibility, laid a few ground rules, and soon it was settled. Pipes would pop my cherry at the Colorado Springs Ramada Inn the day before Thanksgiving. Granted, one Cadet Terry Teason had already burst my technical cherry, but I was still a virgin when it came to girl-on-boy sex.

CHAPTER 22

Pipes had prepaid for the room, so when we got to the Ramada Inn, we went straight from the parking lot to the room. Pipes had convinced someone to buy liquor for him, and a bottle of Beefeater sat next to two liters of 7UP. He mixed our drinks in plastic Ramada Inn cups, and we both drank our liquid courage eagerly, hoping the gin would ease our nervousness.

We sat on the edge of the bed in our academy PT gear like two high school nerds getting ready to play show and touch under the football stadium. Pipes used the TV remote and clicked the channel selector over his shoulder, stopping when he heard soothing classical music. He threw the remote on the other bed, and as he leaned in to kiss me, I saw the weather channel logo fill the screen. I wasn't sure I could go through losing my virginity with the weather channel playing Bach as the seven-day forecast for the Midwest states scrolled across the screen. Of course, officially I had already lost my virginity at Henry's place, but this would be biblical sex, complete with penile penetration.

The thoughts in my head momentarily removed me from what was happening a few inches below, but Pipes's clumsy hands pinched my tits, causing a pain that brought me right back in the moment.

"Sorry." He gulped loudly as I flinched from his touch.

"Not so hard," I instructed like I was some experienced hooker. Based on our candid talks, I had learned that I had touched more boobies than he had. Now that he had fondled mine, I was only up by one pair.

"You touch me," he said with a shaky voice. He pulled my hand toward his blue shorts, and I felt a soft mass beneath.

Assuming he hadn't touched another man's penis besides his own, he and I were now one for one on the number of penises we had touched. I felt like a kid at an exploratorium holding an unfamiliar sea creature. I was surprised at how spongy Pipes's penis felt. Kendra had always talked about stiffies, woodies, and hard-ons, making me believe that it would be firmer.

As if reading my mind, the unfamiliar sea creature began to grow. I wasn't sure what sort of motion it would take to get him where he needed to be, so with a flat hand, I rubbed the front of Pipes's shorts like Aladdin rubbed his magic lamp.

Pipes closed his eyes, leaned back on his hands, and threw his head back in what I perceived to be pleasure. The sea cucumber grew firmer and firmer and I grabbed him through his shorts, amazed at how his penis had gone from squishy to stiffy in less time than the forecaster could predict a hailstorm for the midsection of the country. I was even more amazed that my body was exuding its own signs of approval.

More for my own curiosity than for Pipes's pleasure, I reached beneath his shorts and underwear to make skin-on-skin contact. The heel of my hand was still on Pipes's warm, muscular stomach when my fingers came in contact with thick, curly hair. I ran my fingers through his man bush, confused to feel his stiffness above my hand, apparently ready to spring out from the confines of his briefs.

Pipes moaned even deeper now. He used both hands to push his clothes down to his ankles, and I watched as his penis sprung up and out from his bush. I know thinking it looked like a thick, long-stemmed mushroom with veins wasn't a romantic thought, but it was the first thing that popped in my mind. The mushroom's shaft curved upwards and the large head proportionately capped the shaft.

Kendra, Franny, and I used to ogle *Playgirl* magazines that Kendra somehow got her hands on. I had always assumed that the naked men in those photos were setting us all up for severe disappointment when we encountered the real thing. Having the real thing in front of me at that moment, I struggled to find any disappointment other than wondering how the beast before me was going to find a home inside me.

After Pipes had disrobed his lower half, one hand went back to its tripod support while the other gave a couple slow up-and-down strokes on his penis. I was amazed that I found this to be a turn-on. I mimicked his strokes, still marveling at how his penis could change so quickly from soft to hard.

"That feels so good," Pipes said.

I wanted to continue making him feel good, but I was curious to know what he felt like inside me too. I started with his hand. I gracelessly pulled his hand to me, removing his support without warning and landing him flat on his back. The end justified the means. I crawled to his side and jammed his hand down the front of my shorts.

"Oh wow," he said as he felt the wetness in between my legs. Oh wow was right. His wide, strong fingers and forceful touch felt great. Our mutual strokes were in sync and I gathered that he wanted to be in me as much as I thought I wanted him in me. He and I tugged at my shorts and my freshly shaved crotch earned another, "Oh wow" from Pipes. He pulled me down on top of him and the weight of my body pushed his stiff rod flat against my stomach. Suddenly, Pipes pushed me off. "Shit," he said as he stood up and walked over to the table and grabbed a box of condoms.

Pipes took off his shirt and his hard-on sprung to a horizontal position with a slight bounce, as if a tiny diver had just plunged toward the pool from his springboard dick. He walked back to the bed, tearing into the condom's wrapper. He held out the unwrapped condom. "Do you want to put it on?"

I took it from him, assuming he meant for me to put it on him and was thankful for Kendra's juvenile practices of putting condoms on bananas. Franny and I had giggled like the little girls that we were at the time, but Kendra insisted on holding the instructional class anyway. We went through three condoms each, the first was used for instruction, the second for practice, and third for blindfolded execution and course graduation. Franny had surprised Kendra and shocked me by graduating many-cum-loudly by executing the blindfolded condom application with her mouth.

Pipes sat down, and I rolled the condom onto him as he leaned back on his hands and watched. I realized that if Part P was going into Part V, it would require movement on my part. I stood up and straddled Pipes's lap. His mouth was open as if he weren't actually a participant but only watching. My heart was pounding as I lowered myself and found the sea cucumber had no navigational skills as it poked up through my folds, sliding past the hole it should have entered. Pipes reached down and held still as I came down for a second pass. Mounting the Bone Ranger came with a sharp pain I hadn't expected. Pipe's imprecise lap rocket was heavier weaponry than Terry's gentle precision-guided fingers, and I sat there wondering what the fascination with sex was.

Pipes started to squirm under me like he wanted me off of him. He grabbed my hips and guided me into receiving the clue that he wanted me off of him, then onto him, then off of him, then onto him, all cleverly disguised as an up-and-down motion. I got the hint and worked my legs into a position that facilitated that motion.

The first time I slid myself up his shaft, I got a short break from the painful pressure of his fullness inside me. I also felt the head of his penis catch inside me and it touched something in there that felt better than anything I had ever felt. As I made a less-painful return trip down to his lap again, Pipes whispered, "Warm inside."

I'm not sure what it is about sex, but I realized it incapacitates the ability to form complete sentences as I countered with, "Tip feels good."

We continued our "me Tarzan, you Jane" conversation as I continued to pump up and down. The more cycles I went through, the better the tip of his head felt. I wanted more and so did Pipes. He grabbed me and spun us around, thrusting into me as I lay on my back. His incomplete sentences gave way to grunting, no words, just vowels, "Aaaaaa," and "Oooooo." He pushed himself in and out of me faster and faster with more pain each time. I tried to slide back on the bed to lessen the depth of each plunge, but he shimmied right up with me. I hated being under him, unable to control the movements, unable to stop his forceful thrusts. It was no longer two friends in an endeavor together, but a man racing toward his own finish line pleasure and a woman stuck in the pit, spinning her tires. I tried to bear down like I was holding back pee and that somehow turned him on more and increased his speed a few humps an hour.

"Almost. God. Shit. Here. Now."

I prayed that meant this was almost over and not that he was going to shit right there on the bed.

"Aaaaaaaa."

With the last vowel utterance, his body shook, I felt him shrink inside me, and then he collapsed on top of me. I felt completely and literally unfilled, sexually incomplete, and used. I wasn't sure how I could feel used when I had proposed this whole venture and was clearly using Pipes for an experiment whose results could have been confirmed without this last trial. Nonetheless, I wanted to get out of there.

Pipes was oblivious to my situation. He probably mistakenly thought it was as good for me as it was for him.

"I'm gonna take a shower," I said with a smile as fake as the story I would later tell him about how great it was. I got under the hot water and let the frustration pour off of me. I pulled the showerhead off its base and shot the water up into me. What had started as an attempt to remove the evidence of sex from my insides turned into a delightful discovery of the benefits of a removable showerhead. Once I was able to think clearly, I made up my mind to get out of there.

I left the water running and was pleased to finally see the merits of a bathroom phone, which I used to call Henry. I desperately asked if she could pick me up and if there was room at her table for Thanksgiving the next day.

Pipes was channel surfing in the nude and rushed to cover himself up when I came out of the bathroom wearing the same blue issued shorts and white

USAFA T-shirt I had just shed moments earlier. I gave him a lame story about how I wanted to be alone, how I felt like a different woman and had to "process" everything we had just done. I felt awful lying to him but he said he understood, which made me feel even worse.

"You know, maybe you and I are just better friends than we are—"

"Lovers?" I finished his sentence. I imagine it sounded as foreign to him as it did to me. Pipes and I were academy classmates. We were bonded by survival and necessity, not sex and opportunity.

"This wasn't about us trying to start something as lovers though, was it, Lex?" Pipes asked.

"No," I admitted.

"As long as it doesn't get weird between us," Pipes said.

I agreed, but it wasn't going to happen in an instant, and it wasn't going to happen with me staying there with him.

"I love you, Lex," he said.

"I love you too, Pipes. Thank you."

"No, thank *you*." He smiled and was too relaxed to get out of bed. That was fine by me because I didn't need anything poking at me reminding me what I'd just done.

When Henry picked me up from the Ramada, I wasn't prepared to have to lie to her. She asked me point-blank what was going on.

"Nothing, just missed you and wanted to come over," I tried.

"So you went to see a friend at a hotel, showered there, and decided to call me?"

"I just had sex with a boy," I blurted out. I wasn't sure what compelled me to say it or what I expected Henry's reaction to be, but I felt better after telling her.

"And?"

"And nothing," I said.

It was then that I realized I never wanted to be intimate with a man ever again. Any lingering questions or doubts I had had about my sexuality were now crystal clear to me. I was one hundred percent lesbian.

CHAPTER 23

Henry and I put the stuffed turkey in the oven early enough to fill the house with inviting scents by the time the community started showing up. Cameron was the first familiar person to show up. I was surprised when she walked straight toward me after entering the house. More surprising was the string of about ten guys who followed her through the door. I was afraid of how this would affect the true nature of the party until I saw one pair of men exhibit the first man-on-man kiss I'd ever seen.

"Don't mind them, they'll be drunk, horny, and on their way to a club before dessert," Cameron said, reading my face.

"Happy Thanksgiving, Cam," I said, right before she wished me the same via a moist kiss on the lips.

"Where's Terry? Thought you two were attached at the hip."

"Are you kidding? I just got my uniform; I'm playing the field." It felt good as I said it because I really did feel like the lesbian world was my oyster. Well, clam to be more colloquially correct.

"Well, that's good to hear," Cam said back, although I wasn't entirely sure she was happy because I was available or because Terry was. She pulled two beers from the cooler by the door and seated herself behind me on Henry's deep couch. We talked about random matter, talking more for the mere act of moving our lips. Truth be told, we weren't even talking to each other. I was having a conversation with a guy next to me, and Cameron was talking to a woman sitting on the hassock in front of us.

All that changed the minute Terry walked into the house. Cameron pulled me back against her and whispered in my ear, "I'm having so much fun."

"Yoo-hoo, who ya looking for?" Cameron yelled over the music toward the door where Terry entered. Her search seemed to end when she saw Cameron and me, and she nodded a very casual head lift and sauntered into the kitchen to talk with Henry. Despite sitting with the party's social hub of the moment, I really wanted to be with Terry. I didn't care whether she considered us friends or lovers. I just wanted to be next to her.

I began to make a well-timed exit from Cameron's lap lair when I saw Terry cozy up to a cute brunette sitting on a barstool by the deck. My body remained frozen, but my brain's emotional center was inundated with jealousy as Terry kept perfect eye contact with me while kissing the brunette.

It was too late to continue on my path toward Terry, so I turned around and faced Cameron. Not having thought out exactly what it was I wanted to do, I straddled Cameron, accidentally thrusting my chest into her face. The momentum from the collision sent me backward, causing my arm to reflexively break my fall by propping myself up with one arm on the shoulder of the woman in front of Cameron. My legs were still straddling Cam and now my crotch was elevated to her mouth level thanks to the leverage of the woman behind me. What had started out as an exit from Cameron turned into an awkward, impromptu lap dance that fortunately was well received.

After recovering from my Cirque du Soleil audition piece, I rallied with a more graceful kiss with Cameron, while still keeping a watchful eye on Terry. By now, she had wrapped the brunette's legs around her torso, grabbed the brunette by her ass and slid her closer to her own subtly thrusting body. I stared at Terry in disbelief, feeling like we were in some weird competition and I was losing. Not one to back away from a showdown, I wrapped Cameron's hair in my hand and forced her head even closer to mine, kissing her more firmly than was romantic.

The pressure from our unyielding lip-lock was released by an opposing force tugging at the back of my head. The hair hold brought me to my feet. Henry was now behind me, firmly guiding me, caveman style, to her bedroom, leaving a confused Cameron behind. Without a word, Henry pushed me onto her bed, left the room, and re-entered seconds later with Terry in the same vise grip with which she had delivered me.

"You two better hash out whatever's going on between you," Henry demanded.

The incredulous look on Terry's face matched the one I knew I wore as well.

"Don't give me those looks. Terry, your excessive flirting with the brunette is pushing Lex toward Cameron, the very person I suspect you don't want her near. Watching the two of you try to out-flirt each other is amusing, but I'm not gonna let you do that to each other. So figure it out." Henry left without giving us a chance to defend ourselves to her.

"You can do better than Cameron," Terry said.

"I don't want to be with her, but you're with that brown-haired bimbo. What do you care?"

"If you don't want to be with Cam, then why were you all over her?"

"Again, what difference does it make? You don't want to be with me and—»

"Who said I didn't want to be with you?" Terry cut me off.

"You told Josie we weren't together," I reminded her of her comment the night we had gone to the club.

"Is that what this is about?" Terry asked.

"It's no big deal, just go out and kiss whomever it is you were kissing, I don't give a shit. I really don't."

"It is a big deal. Look Lex, you and I would have trouble making this work. I'm a two degree and—"

"And I'm just a SMACK. Well, I'll keep my eyes out for another SMACK or for someone who's not afraid of associating with one." I got up to leave and Terry pulled me toward her. She kissed me hard and pushed me back onto Henry's bed. Kissing her again was like coming back to your favorite ice-cream flavor after straying to taste the latest and greatest. It was delicious.

When we came out of Henry's room, Terry walked behind me, enveloping me in her arms. Cameron was waiting right outside the door, and Terry kept us moving past her as she sneered, "Maybe next time, Cam."

I didn't get to see what reaction, if any, Cameron had, but Terry whispered in my ear, "She is not happy."

"But your brown-haired bimbo sure seems to be," I said over my shoulder after noticing Terry's previous conquest straddling and kissing another willing participant. Terry was unaffected by her brunette's new partner, and I could only hope that it was because she was with the one she truly wanted: me.

We returned to the holiday festivities, and after a healthy dose of turkey, cranberries, and stuffing, we took part in an overdose of sex. We spent the entire holiday weekend together and a majority of it without clothes. We agreed that at Henry's we could be the couple we wanted to be, and at the Zoo we would be the two degree and SMACK we had to be.

CHAPTER 24

As part of the year-long fraternity pledge process we underwent as fourth-class cadets at the academy, we took part in the age-old tradition of spirit missions. Spirit missions were a cross between four-degree stress relief and revenge. Upperclassmen in your own squadron, typically the three degrees since they wreaked the most havoc on your daily lives, were the targets of spirit missions. They were supposed to be good natured, but sometimes the line between that and malicious got fuzzy.

The time between Thanksgiving and Christmas was laden with the stress of exams and the excitement of winter break. Our decision to do a spirit mission during that time was strategically planned with the knowledge that we'd catch our victims unaware during the normal spirit mission downtime. Since normal spirit missions were accomplished within your own squadron, the other unexpected element was that we teamed up with the SMACKs in the neighboring squadron. Two squadrons shared a square floor plan of cadet rooms, each squadron getting one L-shaped half. While upper-class traffic flowed freely between the squadrons, fourth-class cadets were not allowed to talk in the hallways much less cross the dividing line between squadrons. So, the logistics of tonight's spirit mission was accomplished during class time or during furtive conversations in the bathrooms located on opposite corners of the square.

"Lucky" Cacy, a late adolescent bloomer and former picked-on geek was our primary spirit mission planner. He had creative plans that left the prank victims in awe rather than anger. The post-Thanksgiving, pre-Christmas prank was a simple one: take the three degrees' bathrobes, run them through the showers, and then hang them out to freeze on the air garden trees.

The air garden was about seven hundred feet long and sat on the east quarter of the terrazzo between the two cadet dormitories. The air garden's prominent position in the center of the cadet area was enhanced by its ordered grid of marble strips surrounding rectangles of well-kept grass. Young trees, about ten feet tall, were evenly spaced in each grassy area and were strong enough to bear the weight of a wet bathrobe overnight.

We all met at three a.m. knowing that between two thirty and four a.m., even all-night study groups would have disbanded for a quick hour-and-a-half power nap before last-minute cramming. Lucky divided us into three teams: robe snatchers, robe dousers, and robe hangers. I was on the highest-risk infiltration team, the snatch team. We were charged with the task of taking the two robes of the room's upper-class inhabitants.

The robe-hanging team helped with dismantling the fluorescent light tubes that lit up the hallways so that robe-grabbing teams could go in under complete darkness. Pipes picked me as his partner, and the adrenaline from the task at hand washed away the minimal residual awkwardness from Thanksgiving eve. He held the door slightly ajar as I snuck into our first room, where the three-degree slobs left their closet doors open for easy robe-grabbing access. I grabbed the two robes, flung them one at a time to Pipes, who then tossed them onto team two. With Spirit Mission Robe Freeze underway, we headed to our next assigned room.

We silently invaded eight rooms, stealing sixteen robes. With only two rooms left to go until mission completion, one of the robe-grabbing teams got careless. They made enough noise to wake up the two three degrees in that room, plus the occupants of the neighboring three rooms in the alcove. All hell broke loose as the over-studied, under-slept upperclassmen unleashed their pre-exam fury on our two classmates.

We bolted away from the noise. Robe grabbers and robe dousers fled down the hallway, skidding around corners like cartoon cars up on their outer two wheels. We scattered into the nearest hiding places we could find. A few robe hangers returning from the air gardens for another batch of wet robes quickly caught on to the turn of events and joined the hallway sprints. The one thing that was implicit was that we could not go back to any four-degree room since that'd be the first place the pissed-off upperclassmen would look. We split up and slid into random upper-class rooms, hiding in their closets.

I sat on the closet floor of God knows whose room and discovered another SMACK already in there. Together, we pulled the closet door toward us, leaving a sliver of opening so we could see when the coast was clear. It was hell trying to settle my breath from the unexpected series of sprints we had all just performed. It was even more difficult to do it quietly as we were trying to evade capture.

My classmate slid closer to me, also breathing fast and heavy while trying to be silent. The smell was familiar, but then again, since we were all issued the same brands of shampoo, conditioner, and deodorant, every SMACK smelled like every other SMACK.

"Who is this?" Her hushed, familiar voice breathed against my neck.

"It's Lex. Who's this?" I said, barely able to control my breath much less my volume.

"Mandy," she said.

I hadn't seen much of Mandy since she, Paige, and I helped each other through Jack's Valley. The thought of touching her and tucking in her shirt every day for thirteen days immediately brought back goose bumps. I hadn't thought much about Mandy, but even if I had, I wouldn't have known how to honestly identify the feelings I had about her then. After Terry, after Pipes, after the bar, I knew the feelings I felt were ones of attraction. Not only did I recognize the feelings, but I was finally going to allow myself to feel them.

Due to the very limited space in the closet, I was literally in her lap. Her legs and arms enveloped me only because it was the only way the closet could fit us both and still allow the closet doors to close. While her heart pounded against my back due to the hurried getaway, mine began to pound rapidly because I was wrapped in her arms. I desperately wanted to make a move on her. In the frenzied moment, I thought that I might actually get away with it without Mandy screaming holy homosexuality. But my better judgment kicked in, and I refocused my thoughts.

Even still, I couldn't help but smile at the irony of hiding in the closet with my female classmate.

Both of us jolted upright as someone pounded three times on the room's door. The door flew open, and one of the two degrees from my squadron boomed at the sleepers, "You seen any freshmen come through here?"

"Fuck off," was the sleepy retort from the bed closest to us.

Taking that as a no, the two degree left, and Mandy and I let out a simultaneous silent sigh. I collapsed back against her, and she wrapped her arms tight around me. "Sorry," she whispered into my ear as she released her arm clamps.

Don't be sorry, was my first thought, but all I could manage was to timidly shrug my shoulders.

"What do we do now?" Mandy asked. Her lips brushed against my ear as her warm, moist breath asked a question to which I had myriad inappropriate responses.

I wondered if she could feel the goose bumps that rose on my arms. The curious part of me wished she could and the rational part of me hoped she couldn't. I leaned back to put my mouth close to her ear so I could whisper my response. As I repositioned my body my head hit the hanging clothes above us, clanging empty metal hangers together in a not-so-silent manner. Both sleepers in the room rustled, but neither woke up. We took that as our clue to leave and before we came out of the closet, Mandy brought her face close to mine.

"This was fun, we should do it again sometime," she whispered, her warm breath again rejuvenating the goose bumps on my skin.

My mind interpreted her phrase as an invite, and I felt a magnetic pull toward the lips that uttered the invite. Thankfully, the darkness masked my movement and without giving me a chance to reply, Mandy began to sneak out of the closet. I followed her as if she were the lead lemming guiding me to the cliff's edge. We made it safely to the women's bathroom, and in the bright fluorescent lights of the bathroom, I snapped back from my dream state where Mandy and I were still involved in a passionate kiss.

I caught my reflection in the mirror and shook my head as I realized what I had almost done. I watched Mandy as she frantically checked the shower stalls for any upperclassman who might have been lying in wait to bust us.

"That was awesome!" she said, still trying to keep her volume down since we weren't allowed to talk in the bathrooms.

I tried to herd the butterflies in my stomach that Mandy had let loose and play off excitement over the night's spirit mission. "Yeah," was all the excitement I could gather.

I felt an odd sense of déjà vu as Mandy bent over the toilet stalls to double-check if we were alone. The playful grin on her face when she confirmed that we were truly alone made me think my attempt to kiss her in the closet might have been well received. Mandy strutted toward me and suddenly began the kiss I had envisioned back in the closet.

It was all at once gentle, passionate, fun, and thrilling. Our mouths maneuvered in synchronized motions, a collaborative union of lips that felt like the discovery of a soulmate. Even better was that it felt natural and normal. Illegality of our lip-lock aside, the pleasure of this kiss came from sharing it with a classmate and a friend, someone enduring the same hell as me at the same time.

The bathroom, of all places, seemed to be the make-out place on campus. It wasn't the ideal place for a first kiss, but a homophobic institution didn't offer too many scenic, romantic first kiss locales.

We weren't too far into the kiss when the outer door to the bathroom opened. By the time Paige burst through the second door, Mandy and I were standing apart. Paige was winded from whatever path she had taken when we all scattered, and it was a natural assumption that we were panting for the same reason.

"Hey girls. We better get back to our rooms. The upperclassmen haven't been down to our rooms yet, so if we get in there, they'll never know we were out. Wasn't that fun?"

"No doubt," I said. "I can't wait to do it again." I looked at Mandy, hoping she got my real message.

"Soon, I hope," Mandy said. She got the message.

Paige led the way out of the bathroom. Mandy held the door for me, and as I walked past I skimmed my fingertips across her lower back. She grabbed my hand as it got to her hip and tugged me back toward her. I smiled warningly over my shoulder. "See you soon," I said with a wink.

There was no hope of sleep during what was left of the morning. Thankfully, I didn't have any taxing exams that day because I wouldn't have been able to direct my attention to anything other than Mandy. I managed to pass all my tests and projects but failed when it came to tracking down Mandy before Christmas break.

CHAPTER 25

We had all been counting down the days until Christmas break when we could escape the Zoo. Yet, once freed, I couldn't help but miss the academy. The predictable tranquility of being at home with Mom and Dad was dull compared to the family of one thousand classmate siblings and three thousand upper-class parents telling us what to do every minute of the day.

It was inevitable that Kendra would invite herself over and think she was welcome. Mom sent us off to my room, mistakenly thinking that we girls had "so much catching up to do."

Kendra didn't act like herself. She didn't throw herself on my bed like she belonged there. She didn't start in with her "you're gay and I know it" routine. It wasn't normal, and it made me nervous. She did feel open enough to talk about her first grueling semester of community college and was professing pure exhaustion from her eight credit hours. She was in no mood to hear about my academic load that more than doubled hers, and I was in no mood to try and explain it to her. I was afraid that all she'd want to hear about was my sex life. I was in no mood to try and explain that to her either.

Kendra surprised me by only talking about her sex life. She had allegedly won the coveted "Best Blow Job Giver" award by a panel of six men. While performing great blow jobs gave Kendra, and apparently the six-man panel, great pleasure, it did absolutely nothing for me. I didn't even want to think of putting a penis in or near my mouth, so I let my mind wander off while Kendra extolled the finer points of her technique.

Suddenly, I was back in real time with Kendra looking quizzically at me. "You don't like my technique?"

"What technique?"

"My blow job technique." Apparently, I was in my own little world but I was glad to have missed the blow-by-blow of Kendra's victory.

"I just thought you might be able to use some of those tricks," Kendra said.

I figured "tricks" was the most appropriate word she could have used since she'd blown one man a month since I'd been gone. Not that I wouldn't mind a steady diet of one woman a month, but that was nutritional advice I was going to keep to myself.

"Guess you don't need blow job advice, eh?" Kendra asked.

"Can't hurt," I said with the sarcastic retort of a seemingly seasoned heterosexual.

"I figured with the guy-to-girl ratio there at the academy you would have had to have sex by now." The real Kendra was starting to emerge. I didn't know if I could handle a face-to-face conversation with her about this particular topic.

"Gee Kendra, I'm surprised you think I hooked up with a man."

"Lexy, I'm not going down this path with you. I said all I wanted to say to you when you called me before Thanksgiving. You know how I feel, and you're the one who won't accept you for who you are. Let's just talk about something else. You're only home for two weeks, and I wanna hang out like we used to."

Again, the simple Kendra, flowing smoothly from a conversation about blow jobs to a statement about her unconditional friendship then moving on to the task at hand, which was nothing more than just hanging out.

"Great. I'm ready to have fun too." I didn't have the energy to discuss or chastise Kendra for her matter-of-fact declaration about me being gay. We talked for a while about our new lives and college adventures. It wasn't long before we realized we were now on two very different paths, in more ways than one. We decided to round up Franny and headed out in Kendra's Mustang, and when we roared up in Franny's driveway, she bounced out of her parent's front door. She jumped in the back seat and for a moment, it was as if we were back in high school. The three of us drove to nowhere in particular, singing out loud and off key, enjoying the journey without regard to the destination. The fearsome threesome reunited, if only for a brief time. Our chemistry felt forced, like hanging out together was obligatory.

I knew my mind was on all experiences, opportunities, and challenges that were no longer here at home. I spent my vacation avoiding anything more than superficial conversations, telling my parents what they wanted to hear and my friends what I wanted them to hear.

Christmas break flew by, and in what seemed like hours, not days, it was time to say goodbye to my parents and friends and return to my new life at the academy.

CHAPTER 26

I was glad to get back to the academy, but it seemed as though I was alone in that sentiment. When I landed at the Colorado Springs Airport, several of my classmates were there with eyes swollen from crying. Every pay phone by the baggage carousel was occupied by a uniformed Air Force Academy fourth-class cadet.

"I love you," one cried.

"We'll be together forever," the one next to him blubbered.

The clincher one that made me smile was, "I know, Mommy, but I hate it here and I miss you." It was hard to believe that the guy crying for his mommy would be defending our nation in three and a half short years.

I waited my turn for a phone so I could call Henry for a ride. I didn't have to be back to the Zoo until eight p.m., and my early flight gave me six hours to chill out at Henry's. Having a great sponsor like Henry was a part of why I loved being back in Colorado. It wasn't that I didn't love my parents or didn't miss them. My old life just seemed so boring in comparison to the challenging experiences of my new life.

Seeing Kendra after her first semester of college was a glimpse at what my life might have been like had I not gone to the academy. I realized the experiences I had already gone through and the ones yet to come were an advanced education, not only for my future career, but in life lessons learned. When I graduate, I would walk away with much more than a degree.

My confidence was boosted when I heard Mandy's voice behind me. "Well, I hope you're standing in line to call me to schedule some unfinished business we have." She greeted me with a tight hug and a friendly smile as if we had been friends for years.

"Actually, I'm headed to my sponsor's place. Why don't you come back with me, and we can discuss this unfinished business of which you speak?" I invited her to Henry's without a second thought and without asking Henry. Always a proponent of the more is merrier theory, Henry predictably welcomed Mandy into the Mustang and seemed glad to have a new admirer of her humble abode.

"You girls make yourselves at home. I have to run a few errands, but I'll be home in time to get you back by eight."

Mandy shot me a mischievous grin that I hoped meant she was thinking the same thoughts I was about being alone together. We wasted several minutes on small talk about Henry as my sponsor and how dull our Christmas breaks had been. Then I surprised myself with my bravado as I said, "Should we get back in the closet or the bathroom to finish what you started, or can we resume it right here?"

The words "no time like the present" were implied in Mandy's powerful kiss. It was the kind of kiss reserved for couples reunited at airports after months apart. In our case, it was the kind of kiss reserved for two chicks who couldn't get away with this kind of kiss anywhere else. Mandy had no reservations about kissing another woman, and it seemed that I didn't either. The kiss led us downstairs to my room. After all, we weren't animals who had to do it right there on the couch. Although, I had been that animal on that couch with Terry.

How we made it down the flight of stairs, through the hallway, and into the room while never losing full-lipped contact was beyond me. We finally landed on the bed in a tangled weave with Mandy on top. I rolled her over and tried to continue the kiss with her underneath me. That was exactly what Mandy had in mind, and she rolled us over again, putting me underneath her. We were like a lip-lock rotisserie, me on top, Mandy on top, me on top.

As we teetered on the edge of the bed, Mandy managed to break free from the kiss to smile and say, "You're a top."

Having never heard this expression before, I assumed she was referring to our slightly dizzying spin of kissing revolutions. So when I said, "Just like a dreidel," it made sense to me, but not to Mandy. Mandy realized that my knowledge of lesbian life and lingo was limited. She went on to explain the more dominant role of the "top" and the more receiving nature of the "bottom." Then she questioned my gay qualifications. "Have you been with a woman before or is this your first kiss?"

"Of course I've been with women. I've been with six," I lied. I said "been with" but meant "kissed" and the six included Kendra, Terry, Cameron, Henry, and Mandy twice because it helped my numbers.

Despite having five references to vouch for my homosexual tendencies, failing the top-bottom knowledge test caused Mandy to throttle back on her advances. Instead, we talked about past exploits: where we'd done it, how we'd done it, but not whom we'd done. Mandy talked about her escapades during high school, and she literally meant during high school.

"I got a small piece of action once during a home economics class. We had finished our apron assignment before everyone else and while she tried on her apron, I tried her on under her apron. Perfect fit."

We went one for one, swapping stories. I had to assume hers were true but failed to admit that mine were pure fiction. We had a very natural rhythm of banter that was both playful and seductive. I was impressed with my impromptu tales but wanted at least one to be true.

"Did I tell you about our classmate I hooked up with?" I started.

"No. Do tell." Mandy scooted forward, sitting Indian style on the bed.

"Totally hot. In fact, it happened right here on this very bed. She was pretty shy, so I started slowly. Just a kiss at first. You know, to see how she'd react." I leaned forward and kissed Mandy softly on the lips. Mandy kissed me back, quickly getting the idea.

"Then what?"

I continued, "The kiss was well received, so I made sure she was comfortable and moved to give the girls some attention," as I pushed Mandy to a prone position and nuzzled her breasts. She proved to be an attentive listener as I unwove my fable, making it true with my tongue. I was getting closer to the climax of my story, though few words were being spoken, when I heard Henry returning from her errands. We both snapped up realizing that we would once again have unresolved business. Mandy pulled up her pants and buttoned up her shirt as I flipped on the TV. We lay back on the bed trying to pull off innocence, despite the scent of guilt that filled the room.

There were three surprised faces for three different reasons when Terry walked into my bedroom. Mandy was shocked to see Cadet Teason. I was surprised it wasn't Henry. Terry was confused by my current bedmate. Terry was at a loss for words, turned, and slammed the door shut. Mandy was at a loss for thought when I told her I'd be right back and left after Terry.

"Hey, welcome back. D'ya have a good Christmas?" I said as I barged into Terry's room.

"I see you found a SMACK."

"Yeah, to hang out with. What's the big deal?"

"Smells like you've been hanging out kind of low." Terry brushed past me and left me standing there in her room. I felt numb and just stared at her bed where her suitcase and backpack sat. On top of the backpack was a small, wrapped box with a gift tag that clearly indicated it was to me and from Terry, with love. I felt awful.

I sulked back into my room thinking I could pull off the incident without an explanation. Wishful thinking. Mandy's open mouth allowed a stream of questions to flood out.

"Was that Cadet Teason? Do you two have the same sponsor? Is she…have you two…are you still…?" Mandy's questions hung in the air and then answered themselves in the silence. I waited for her to storm out of the room. What I got instead was a whole new line of questioning.

"How is she? She's a top, isn't she? Does she yell at you in the sack? How long have you guys been doing it? Tell me all the places you've done it at the Zoo." Mandy's pace of questioning was impossible to keep up with even though I had no intention on answering any of the questions. I just smiled.

"Holy shit. This is huge. I can't believe you're making it with a two degree! You must be amazing in bed. I mean I got a little taste of it, well, you did the tasting, but man! Teason could get kicked out of the Zoo for doing you. You must be worth it." Mandy's speaking volume now matched her conversational pace, and I had to put my hand over her mouth to shut her up. Her head and my hand shook side to side as her eyes reflected a newfound respect for whatever talent she thought I possessed to make Terry hook up with me.

I'd never really given much thought to what Terry or I risked. She had a lot more to lose than her reputation. If you quit or got kicked out of the academy even one minute beyond the first day of your two-degree year, you owed the Air Force time or money in repayment for the first two years of school. Whatever her motivation was, she had more in jeopardy than I did.

"You know you can't say anything, Mandy," I stated the obvious.

"I know, but you gotta tell me more," she said anxiously.

I was tempted to brag, but I took the high road and kept sex between me and Terry between me and Terry.

CHAPTER 27

Terry left Henry's house during Mandy's inquisition and hadn't returned by the time Henry drove Mandy and me back to school. By then, my stomach was a churning volcano of acid, ready to erupt. I wanted to find Terry and make everything all right, but I was back in the academy life and would not get that chance anytime soon.

"Hey, let's meet at the Arnold Hall pizzeria after we both sign in to our squadrons." Mandy's peppiness revealed her lack of perceptiveness and inability to recognize my turmoil.

"Yeah, sure." My reply was 180 degrees from her enthusiasm.

I signed in, dropped off my suitcase in my room, and convinced Paige to join me in a chilly stroll to the pizzeria. We had to put on our overcoats, scarves, and gloves because while Colorado in January at sea level was cold, Colorado in January a mile up was fucking freezing. Mandy met up with Paige and me just as we were exiting the building to rush across the terrazzo toward Arnold Hall. The three of us were literally skidding along the icy marble strips that defined the inefficient route of travel fourth-class cadets were mandated to take. The blustery wind used our bulky overcoats as sails to propel us faster than our legs could carry us. As dictated by Murphy's Law, Cadet Teason was returning to the squadron as we skidded by.

"Good evening, Cadet Teason," all three of us shouted in unison.

I'm not sure what expression Mandy wore, given her newfound discovery, but I knew that utter fear was all over my face. Whatever she saw or felt caused Cadet Teason to stop all three of us.

"Where the fuck do you think you girls are going?" Cadet Teason slurred.

"Ma'am, we are going to Arnold Hall," shouted Paige.

"Seivers, get out of here," Cadet Teason shouted.

Paige hesitated for a moment. From the corner of my eye, I could see Mandy grab Paige's hand to stop her from leaving. Paige was torn between obeying Cadet Teason's order and abandoning her classmates, so she stood frozen with Mandy's hand on her own.

"You better pick a classmate, Roberts," Cadet Teason hissed.

"Ma'am, may I make a statement?" I yelled to be heard over the whipping winds.

"Cadet Eerie Cat, if I were you, I'd plead the fifth on the grounds that what you may be about to say may incriminate you," Cadet Teason bellowed. She seemed to get more coherent the angrier she got.

Paige violated fourth-class decorum and looked at me and Mandy with an even more confused look on her face, if that was possible.

"On second thought," Cadet Teason continued, "all three of you stooges get out of my sight before I report you for disobedience and disrespect. Do I make myself clear?"

Without the proper, "Yes, ma'am," the three of us sprinted away from Cadet Teason and her tirade.

"Man, Cadet Teason must have had a pissy Christmas," Paige said as we made it to the safety of Arnold Hall.

"Maybe she had to share one of her presents," Mandy said. Her double entendre did not pass me by.

"That'd be a weird reason to be in a pissy mood," Paige said as the double meaning flew over her.

"I wish we could have a drink," I said, partly in truth but mostly to switch subjects. I could see the upperclassmen in the Arnold Hall sports bar, drinking themselves warm. I imagined that the sports bar was Terry's first stop after leaving Henry's. It wasn't hard to imagine after smelling a few beers on her breath and hearing the slur in her speech.

"What would you have?" Paige asked as if her enthusiasm would materialize drinks.

"Sex on the beach." Mandy smiled at Paige and raised her eyebrows a couple times.

"Ooooh, that sounds yummy," Paige squealed. She was missing more than she realized.

We continued our Christmas break recaps while we sat scrunched together at the small round table outside the sports bar. Paige felt comfortable enough to share her most recent exploits with her FTF back home. Mandy felt bold enough to share our most recent exploit substituting male for female pronouns. Mandy's story expanded beyond where the actual story had been interrupted as if to put the possibility on the table. Meanwhile, under the table, Mandy's leg slid in between mine, our inner thighs making complete contact beneath the dark-blue tablecloth. Mandy had the amazing ability to carry on an intelligible conversation while caressing my leg with hers. Paige had the expected ability to be oblivious to it all.

I was grateful that Mandy's recent discovery about whatever was going on between Terry and me wasn't enough to stop her from pursuing something between us. I wanted to keep my options open, although I couldn't deny the inexplicable pull to Terry, but I didn't know if it was the power of having an upperclassman's private attention or Terry herself that I was attracted to. But there was something poetic about a budding relationship with Mandy, a classmate enduring the same hell and limitations with me. And if her tales of experience were true, she was also a perfect guide into this new world I finally realized I wanted.

We stayed for about an hour, chatting with random classmates who needed to be cheered up now that we were all re-incarcerated at the prison we called school. When we had reached our limit of listening to our classmates' whining, we decided it was time to head back to our respective squadrons. I wasn't thrilled about heading back to the squadron for fear of seeing Cadet Teason or worse yet, dealing with her wrath of jealousy. Fortunately, she wasn't in the path between Arnold Hall and my room, and I returned unscathed.

CHAPTER 28

The thirty-two of us SMACKs stood in the squadron's hallways in groups of two or three preparing to shout out the countdown to pre-breakfast festivities. Every morning, the academy's entire cadet body formed up by squadron on the terrazzo, saluted proudly during the playing of "Reveille" and the raising of the American flag, then marched in an orderly fashion into our chow hall, also known as Mitchell Hall. Just the same as the first semester, there were ten-minute, seven-minute, and five-minute countdowns, and our callouts would be in perfect sync with the other squadron's SMACKs on our floor. Typically, in between the ten- and seven-minute calls, we ran back to our rooms to cram more knowledge into our heads. As this was the first morning back to the academy after our Christmas break, we had no reason to believe it would be any different than the mornings before break.

Lucky stood at the Cadet in Charge of Quarters desk. "Roadrunners, prepare to call the tenth minute," he said in normal conversational volume. This was like a band conductor's preparatory wand wave as we inhaled for our announcement. "Roadrunners! There are ten minutes until first call for the morning meal formation. Uniform is: athletic jackets, flight caps, and gray leather gloves. The menu for the morning meal includes: bacon, eggs, toast, and orange juice. There are ten minutes until first call."

As soon as we had completed our broadcast, upperclassmen poured out of their rooms and unleashed an unusual barrage.

"You make me sick! Can't you guys get it in unison?" yelled one.

"You all go home to your mommies and daddies and get all soft and forget everything you've learned about teamwork. You suck!" yelled another.

Insults and attacks came from every direction about how we'd fallen apart over the break and how we'd better get our shit together or else we wouldn't make it to spring break. We just stood there in our groups, taking the abuse, not because we agreed with them, but because they weren't asking any sort of knowledge questions. We were dumbfounded by the undeserved lashings. It was a common consensus that everyone hated being back, but the upperclassmen had fourth-class punching bags for their emotions. They spent a few minutes landing verbal jabs on us since we were defenseless by nature of the academy's rank structure. As quickly as the storm had blown in, a rapid calm settled and the upperclassmen, mostly three degrees, paced in front of us.

Cadet Tollet, the primary cadet in charge of training, broke the silence. "I hope you all had a nice break." I sensed some insincerity. "But you better realize that you're back now and that means you belong to me until recognition."

Recognition was the formal ceremony that would reward our hard work from Basic Cadet Training through the entire four-degree year and "recognize" us as normal academy cadets. It was preceded by hell week but came after spring break, which was still a lifetime away in fourth-class cadet time.

"So just to reorient you to academy life, we're going to host a training session tonight at eighteen hundred hours in the squadron assembly room. I suggest you brush up on your knowledge, get your shit together, and show me you even deserve to be recognized." The other three degrees continued to pace, glaring at us as if we had committed a crime more heinous than not shouting in unison.

Cadet Tollet went up to Lucky and asked in a mockingly pleasant tone, "How many minutes until first call for the morning meal formation?"

Lucky robotically looked at his digital Casio watch and replied, "Sir, there are six minutes until first call for the morning meal formation." You could hear Lucky's tone of voice drop when he realized that in all the shouting about how much we sucked, we had missed the seven-minute call for the morning formation. This fact was not lost on Cadet Tollet.

"This is exactly what I'm talking about, you worthless pieces of shit! We train your sorry asses for five months, then you go home for two weeks and come back and can't remember a goddamn thing. What fucking good are you people? I can't believe—"

"Roadrunners!" in unison, without prompting, we all yelled at the top of our lungs, "There are six minutes until first call for the morning meal formation. Uniform is: athletic jackets, flight caps, and gray leather gloves. The menu for the morning meal includes: bacon, eggs, toast, and orange juice. There are six minutes until first call."

The call for the fifth and final minute came shortly after, and we all scurried out to the terrazzo to salute the flag and march to breakfast. For those who missed their mommies, there was no more time to be homesick.

There also wasn't much time to focus on reading assignments by the time the end of the academic day rolled around. The thirty-two of us crowded into Pipes's room as we did our normal training session preparations. We shined our glossy shoes and quizzed each other on our memorization of quotes from *Contrails*. That night, we added a new step to our preparations by eating copious amounts of bad breath–producing food products. Bags of Dorito chips, garlic-flavored pretzels, and onion-rich salsa circulated the room. We also pounded back as many carbonated drinks as we could in the hopes that the bubbles would help the stench of garlic and onions surfacing from our bellies. When it was time for us to march ourselves down to the squadron assembly room, our stomachs were indeed grumbling from the contents we had ingested.

The curtains on all four sides of the glass assembly room were pulled shut, and there was condensation on the inside of the windows. As we entered the room from the terrazzo level, a wall of intense heat hit us that contrasted with the cold evening air. The upperclassmen were already in there. They had given the room ample time to warm up to what must have been more than ninety degrees. Despite arriving three minutes before six p.m., they let us know we were late. The upperclassmen didn't need an excuse to unload their tensions on us in the form of "training" us to be great Air Force officers, but whatever their justification, we belonged to them for the next hour.

Common strategies to test our teamwork hadn't changed, and an upperclassman or cluster of upperclassmen would try to isolate one of us from the pack and ride us until fellow SMACKs came to the rescue. SMACK rescues were sometimes simple acts like sandwiching the lone victim and shouting unsolicited quotes or academy factoids. More theatrical rescues involved several fourth classmen in a single file line weaving toward the separated classmate, thumping their fists on their chests to imitate helicopter rotors pounding the air. The rescue chopper line would push upperclassmen aside, encircle the downed SMACK, and whisk him away from the torturous interrogators. There was no need for rescue choppers tonight because every single one of us was pulled away from classmate support and privy to a one-on-one training session in the sweltering heat.

Although we were each alone with two or three of our very own upper-class bastards, we projected teamwork through throat-ripping loudness. That loudness reeked of not only teamwork, but of an overpowering Italian kitchen. The furious carbonation combination of Coke, Pepsi, and root beer helped propel the stench to our captive audience, and at one point I heard a classmate let loose a royal, eye-watering, award-winning belch.

"OH MY GAWD!" yelled one of his personal trainers.

Impervious to our own stink, we continued spouting off quotes and general fourth-class knowledge. Upperclassmen exhibited quick thinking and turned their particular four degree to face the thick curtains while continuing their assaults from behind. We stood facing the curtains like lost, blind children with Tourette syndrome. The voices changed frequently as upperclassmen took turns harassing different SMACKs.

"Well, well, well, Eerie Cat, guess you're all alone now, eh?" Cadet Teason's voice was the only one I could hear directly behind me.

"Yes ma'am," I shouted to the curtain.

"I bet you miss your little buddy, don't you?"

"No ma'am."

"Did you guys have fun at Henry's? Do you sneak into each other's rooms at night? Are you playing me? You think you're hot shit getting away with nailing an upperclassman and a classmate?" Cadet Teason was talking right into my ear. She was talking just loud enough for me to hear, but the edge in her voice was no different from any other upper-class ass in the room. Her chest was pressed against my back and sweat-soaked shirt as she abused her upper-class upper hand to release her jealousy. As sadomasochistic as it was, my shirt was not the only thing getting drenched.

"You gonna answer me, Eerie Cat? Do you guys sneak into each other's rooms? Do you think I don't know what goes on after taps?" She was stabbing in the dark, and we both knew it.

"No ma'am," I shouted. I leaned back into her, feeling both of her tits against my back. When she didn't push me away, the temperature in the room rose several more degrees.

"Lex, don't. We can't." Her tone of voice changed.

"Yes ma'am," I shouted, more for the sake of just shouting something. I leaned into her, and she leaned back.

"How about you sneak into my room after taps sometime?" Cadet Teason whispered.

"Ma'am, I do not know." A fourth-class cadet in an upperclassman's room would be a hard one to explain to her roommate or anyone else who might catch us.

"Just play along," Terry said. Then she jammed her right hand between my elbow and rib cage. Upperclassmen were always making similar flat-handed pokes at us to make sure that our arms were "pinned" against our sides. It was a part of the fourth-class cadet posture of "chin in, shoulders back and down, chest out, stomach in, arms pinned." Many times, an upperclassman would hold their hand at your side, daring you to release pressure on it. That's precisely what Terry was doing then, except her fingertips stroked the side of my breast, again raising the room's temperature.

"Does that feel good?" Terry purred.

"Yes ma'am."

Her left hand assumed the same position on my other side, her fingers grasping a more generous share of my left tit. I leaned farther back into her.

"Is this what you want?" she asked.

"Yes ma'am."

"Then stop fooling around with the SMACK. I can give you more than she can," Terry said curtly.

"Yes ma'am."

Terry pulled her hands away from my sides and thrust her chest forward to give me some forward momentum before she pulled herself away as my physical support. The male voice that replaced hers resumed the quote-requesting screamfest from which he thought Cadet Teason had just walked away. I dutifully and accurately hollered out my memorized knowledge to his liking, and he took it easy on me for the tail end of the training session.

We were dismissed after an hour in the sauna, and while we traversed the outdoor route to the stairwell, the upperclassmen took the more direct elevator route back to the squadron living area. By the time we made it up the stairs to the fifth floor, my nipples were frozen nubs that protruded through my wet, blue uniform shirt.

The upperclassmen lined the hallways as we quietly went back to our own rooms. I obeyed the proper fourth-class cadet posture as I walked, my chest having gained a couple centimeters from the cold. Passing by Cadet Teason, I watched her eyes drop their gaze to my chest. When her eyes came back up to meet mine, there was a smile on her face. Risking a warranted ass chewing, I winked at her. Lucky for me, Terry was the only one who saw it, or the only one who acknowledged seeing it, and replied with a bigger smile.

CHAPTER 29

The second semester of my fourth-class year was zipping by. Aside from the normal academic hell, there were only two things to hurdle before being recognized as a semi-human academy cadet: spring break and recognition. Spring break was the pleasure before the pain of hell week, which ended with recognition. Recognition would signify our official end to being treated as a fourth-class cadet.

I had no extravagant plans for spring break. Most of my classmates were dead set on getting as far from the Zoo as possible. Truth was, I didn't hate the Zoo. I was doing well academically, athletically, and militarily. Hell, even my sex life was thriving by SMACK standards. I didn't really want to fly home to spend my week off with my parents, so in lieu of spending the nights in the dorms, I accepted Henry's invitation to stay at her place during the week. I was sure that Terry would be part of the get-the-hell-out-of-dodge contingent, so I'd have Henry and Henry's place to myself.

"Eerie Cat!" a voice hollered through my door. A single knock followed and then the door came flying open. I couldn't help but think how much I was looking forward to some increased privacy after recognition. "Phone call," said the voice, whose body was already walking back to the Cadet in Charge of Quarters desk. I could only hope that upper-class manners would be part of the recognition package.

My first thought was that something had happened to one of my parents because fourth-class cadets rarely got phone calls. As I approached the Cadet in Charge of Quarters desk, the three degree pointed toward a small room with three pay phones, indicating my call was in there. That was even more unusual. I didn't even know those phones were capable of incoming calls. Tentatively, I slid into the only open phone booth, standing at attention but sliding the door shut, trapping myself into the musty booth.

"Lex?"

"Yeah," I answered tentatively, unable to place the voice.

"It's Terry."

Confusion prevented a reply.

"Are you there?"

"Yes ma'am," I whispered.

"Knock it off. How are you?" Terry said.

"Fine? Where are you? Why are you calling me here? And why are you whispering?"

"I'm at Henry's, and I'm not sure why I'm whispering." Terry's volume increased to normal. "Henry just told me that you were going to spend spring break here."

"Yeah."

"Are you bringing anyone with you?"

"No."

"You're not bringing Roberts?"

"Terry, I told you, we're not like that. I'm coming alone."

"Prove it."

"Prove what?" The conversation was going nowhere fast.

"Prove that you're not with Roberts. Prove it by spending spring break with me at Henry's. I'm not leaving town either, and I'd like to see you again."

Since Terry saw me every day, I translated "see" as "have sex," which was fine by me. "Okay."

"Cool," Terry said with a relieved voice, "I'll see you tomorrow."

I got off the phone but kept myself inside the phone booth until I could compose myself for the walk back to my room. It felt good to be wanted and even better to have a week with Terry on the horizon.

CHAPTER 30

The Friday before spring break crept by at an excruciatingly slow pace. I couldn't wait to get to Henry's, throw on some civilian clothes, and then throw them off to be with Terry. Henry picked me up at the base of the Bring Me Men ramp and seemed as excited as me about my week off.

"Terry's already home, so the door should be unlocked. I need to go to the grocery store for tonight's barbecue." Henry pulled into her driveway and waited for me to get out. As she backed out of the driveway, Terry opened the front door and took my backpack from me.

Without a word, she attacked me with an eager kiss. "God, I missed kissing you," she said after taking away my supply of oxygen.

I had no reply other than a counter kiss with a double-handed ass grab. Calling the kiss and grab foreplay, we ripped at each other's clothes as we stumbled our way down to Terry's bed, selected only because it was the closest. The only thing I was wearing by the time we got there was one black sock and a watch. Terry was completely naked and clean shaven.

As we stood at the edge of her bed, I planted my right hand firmly on her pussy and my entire mouth firmly on her left breast. Terry threw her head back and held my head to her chest as she pulled us both back onto the bed. I thrust my well-saturated thumb inside her, catching her off guard as she moaned in delight. She bent her left knee, giving me deeper access into her, while she began to stroke me with her right hand. Our long-awaited sex was not gentle or patient and neither were our orgasms.

"Fuck, Lexy, that's what I needed," Terry said breathlessly.

I only kissed her because I wanted another round. I flipped her over and laid myself on top of her before she could get her breath back. Once again, I slipped my thumb into her, this time giving my other fingers access to her clit.

"Oh God," Terry managed to say.

"Does that feel good?" I murmured into her ear like she had done to me only weeks before. It was empowering to mount her and have her submit to my desires. She came quickly a second time then wilted beneath me. Our sweaty bodies clung together until we parted with a noisy squish. She rolled onto her back and I played with her still-erect nipples.

"Bring my dinner down here, I can't move," she laughed.

"Yes, your majesty. Anything else I can do for you?" I teased back.

"Ask me later."

We took a leisurely shared shower and were dressed and on our second beers by the time Henry came home. The three of us made hamburger patties and had just thrown them on the grill when Henry dropped a bomb on me.

"Your two high school friends will be here Sunday night to spend the week here." Henry's voice was high pitched and giddy.

"What two friends?" I asked. It seemed that it was the same question Terry was getting ready to ask me.

"Kendra and Franny," Henry said. "We've been planning it for weeks!"

I shook my head in disbelief as Henry explained how she and Mom had coordinated this surprise for me. Henry looked defeated and asked why this didn't appear to be good news. I was forced to tell them both about Kendra's persistent accusations and my consistent denials, or at least my omissions of agreement. I chose to leave out the part about the truth or dare game that had started the accusation.

"So just tell Kendra you're gay," Terry said.

"It's not that easy," I started, but then realized I didn't know why I hadn't told Kendra or why I felt I couldn't tell Kendra. I felt sure of who I had become, or who I always had been, and I was even more certain that Kendra was sure of who I was. But somehow the thought of uttering that adjective in reference to myself seemed so difficult, so final. One thing was for sure: I didn't want to deal with it this week.

"Why did they have to come this week? All I wanted to do was chill out here with you guys," I said. Henry, Terry, and I all knew that "chill out" meant "sex" and "you guys" meant "Terry."

Kendra and Franny's visit would complicate the week or force me into a decision point of admitting what Kendra already knew and what Franny wouldn't figure out if she walked in on me and Terry naked.

A knot wrenched on my stomach as I struggled to figure out why my loyalty to a woman I had known for less than a year was stronger than my loyalty to friends I'd known for more than a decade.

CHAPTER 31

Kendra and Franny were as impressed with Henry's house as I had been the first day I saw it.

"Oh wow, this is wonderful," Franny squealed. Her voice went up two octaves and her *wonderful* had eight *o*'s.

"You have nothing to bitch about if this is where you come after school," Kendra said, showing off her ignorance about my schedule as a SMACK.

We dragged their bags down to my bedroom, and we all stared at the queen-sized bed. *This will be fun,* I thought with a great deal of sarcasm.

"This will be fun," Franny said, with a great deal of excitement.

"This *will* be fun," Kendra said, with a hint of suggestion and a teasing smile aimed at me.

Henry put her arm around Franny's shoulder. "Franny told me on the phone how much she missed your high-school sleepovers, so I figure you'll make this bed situation work. If not, there's a comfy couch upstairs."

Terry slid away from the group, and the only notice I had that she was gone was the sound of her bedroom door quietly shutting. Franny's desire to tell us how bad she had to pee was finally overcome by actually doing something about it. Kendra plopped down on the bed and laid claim over the remote control. Henry disappeared upstairs, and I let myself into Terry's room.

"So much for our spring break, huh?" I asked.

"Yeah, especially if your friends don't know who you really are," Terry said from her outstretched position.

"What am I supposed to do, tell them just so we can fuck around?"

"Or so that they'll know the real you and love you just the same."

I wasn't in the mood to hear Terry lecture me, so I went back and watched TV with Kendra. Franny was due out of the bathroom at any moment, so I knew Kendra wouldn't start a conversation we couldn't finish in front of Franny.

I was wrong.

"Terry's cute," Kendra said.

"Okay," I said.

"Is she a good kisser?"

"Fuck you, Kendra. If you're going to be this way the entire week, then you should just leave now. This is my only week off, and I don't need your shit." I was pissed. Pissed that Kendra was here and ruining my week with Terry. And pissed that she knew me so well.

Kendra rolled over on her stomach, propped herself up on her elbows, and looked me dead in the eyes. "Lexy. I love you. If Terry's important to you, then me and Franny wanna get to know her. Why does that make you so fucking pissy? Is she the upperclassman who was interested in you back at Thanksgiving?"

Thankfully, Franny chose that moment to be done with her bathroom journey. "What are you two talking about?"

"Well," Kendra started, "I was thinking about dog piling Lexy since we haven't seen her in forever!" Kendra rolled on top of me and soon Franny's weight was added. We tickled each other and laughed as we wrestled on the bed. Terry tried to be stealthy as she opened her door to find the root of the commotion, but Kendra caught her and halted the wrestling match.

"Terry! Come on in here. Lexy's told us so much about you. I was more excited to come and meet you than to see Miss Alexis here." Kendra was a lying schmoozer.

Terry accepted the welcome and suggested we all go upstairs and get a beer. Kendra held up her beer and made a toast to new friends and a great week. I stared at her, awestruck at how comfortably she fit in. She was a natural socialite, making easy conversation with Terry and Henry, both of whom laughed at her witty sense of humor. We all put away too many beers, but I was careful about drinking my lips loose. Franny and Kendra were handicapped by the time difference, jet lag, and their inexperience with high-altitude drinking and were therefore the night's first casualties.

Terry and I walked the two of them down to the bed and tucked them in. Franny was out cold, but Kendra was more coherent than she led on.

"Lexy, there's no room in here for three of us. You sleep with Terry," Kendra slurred.

"All right. Good night. I'm glad you guys are here." I pulled the covers up tighter around Kendra.

Kendra pulled me closer so she could slur some secret. "I like her. She's cute," Kendra revealed in a loud voice.

When I saw the smile on Terry's face, I smiled.

"Okay, Ken, go to sleep." I pulled away from her drunken grip.

"Gimme a good night kiss, Lexy."

"No, Kendra. Go to sleep."

"Please. I love you," Kendra pleaded.

"No, you lightweight. Go to sleep."

"Come on, Lexy, you're such a good kisser. Gimme one." Kendra's voice was trailing off, leading me to believe that extended deterrence would make me the victor.

"How 'bout a good night kiss from me?" Terry was behind me with her hands on my hips, talking over my shoulder.

"Fuck yeah, I'll take a kiss from you," Kendra said in a sleepy voice as her eyebrows strained to pull her eyelids open.

Terry leaned over, still holding my hips, now for balance, and planted a gentle kiss on Kendra's forehead.

Kendra was satisfied with the attention, and a lazy smile crossed her face. "You guys look really good together." Then she drifted off into a comatose sleep.

Terry and I tiptoed out of the room, softly closing the door as if we were parents who had just put our kids to bed. I thought we were headed into her room, but she redirected us upstairs to the living room. Henry was still up, surfing through late night TV.

"Wanna join us in the hot tub?" Terry asked.

"That sounds good. I'll meet you out there. Grab the Carnival." The carnival code was cracked when Terry retrieved a bottle of white wine from the fridge.

The white label was festive with balloons and the name Carnival scripted across it. I grabbed three wineglasses while Terry convinced the cork out of the bottle.

"What was that whole ‹beer before liquor› jingle you taught me?" I asked, skeptical about drinking any more alcohol.

"The hot tub voids all drinking rules. This wine is like dessert."

We all went to get into our swimsuits, and soon after Terry and I got to the hot tub, Henry emerged through the French doors from her bedroom with three body towels. I held out a full glass of Carnival for her.

Terry and Henry wasted no time donning the cloak of steam from the hot tub. I followed. My skin had adjusted to the nippy night air and descending into the blistering water felt as if I were being scalded. The chilled wine helped as I lowered myself into the cauldron. The wine was refreshing nectar that tasted like peach-flavored Jolly Rancher candies.

"Your friends seem comfortable here," Henry said.

"I was thinking the exact same thing," I replied.

"I take it you told them?" Henry asked.

"No but—"

"I'm thinking Kendra knows," Terry cut me off. She went on to tell Henry what had happened downstairs.

She pulled me into her embrace, displacing water over the side of the tub and wine over the side of my glass. Her cold wineglass lay against my hot skin as she leaned across the tub to brag, saying, "Kendra thinks I'm cute and that we look good together."

"Well, you are cute, and you two do look good together," Henry laughed.

"You should just tell them, Lex. They don't seem like they care," Terry said.

"I don't know." I was too tired to talk about it and well on the way to being too drunk to care.

"I mean, if they saw us now, they'd figure it out," Henry started. "Rub a dub dub, naked lesbians in a tub."

"Henry, no one's naked," I reminded her of what I thought was obvious.

"Well, I'm on my way there," Henry said. Suddenly from the shallow depths of the hot tub, Henry's non-wineglass hand splashed forth, holding the bottoms of her bikini. She giggled and flung her bikini bottoms down the length of the deck where they landed with a sodden smack. While I was watching the flight of the bikini bottom, I caught the airborne flight of a matching swatch of fabric. Its flight was abruptly interrupted, and soon Henry's bikini top hung neatly from the deck's light.

I was in the middle of registering what I was looking at when Henry's giggling became louder.

I turned to see Henry's tits bobbing in the hot tub, jiggling in perfect tempo with her laughs. Terry was fidgeting behind me and before long, I was the only clothed one in the tub.

Maybe it was the wine, maybe it was the beer, maybe it was the altitude. No matter what the cause, the result was me feeling the need to stand up and ceremoniously join the bare-in-the-tub club. I stood up in the middle of the tub and hooked my thumbs in the sides of my swimsuit bottom. I seductively slid the suit down, worked my feet out of the holes and let my suit join the rest of the clothes down at the other end of the deck. Unsteadied by the tub's powerful jets, surely it couldn't have been the alcohol, I let Terry's hands guide me back down to her lap. I less ceremoniously removed my top and pitched it backward. Momentary silence was soon followed by the rustling of tree branches and all three of us stood up to verify what we already knew.

My bra top waved gently from the treetop below, causing an uproar of laughter. Knowing there was no way for us to get it back made us laugh hysterically. It took us the rest of the bottle of wine to stop laughing.

Terry curled her legs over my thighs and behind my calves, forcing my legs to spread wider than was appropriate. In her drunken state, Terry slid her hand in between my leg, thinking Henry, in her drunken state, wouldn't notice. It didn't matter what state I was in, it felt good and I wasn't going to do a damn thing to stop Terry's hand.

Henry stretched her legs out, and her feet ended up on my knees. I grabbed her feet and massaged them. I could feel Terry's chest rise and fall faster and deeper and her breaths matched her hand's motion on me. The strength and pace of my touch on Henry's feet soon reflected Terry's deep, rapid breathing.

"You guys are making me horny, and that's my cue to leave." Henry stood up, disrupting the chain of touches we had.

"So, stay in here," Terry suggested.

Henry pulled in a deep, thoughtful breath. "Ask me again in about three years," she said as she exhaled. Public math would have told me that in three years, all of us would have graduated from the Zoo, me being the limiting one. Public math with alcohol left me wondering why three years instead of two or four. I was still running the beads on my mental abacus while Henry went back in the house and Terry resumed her underwater crotch stroke.

"You ever done a three way?" Terry asked.

"I think it's safe to say that I haven't. Have you?"

"Only in my dreams." Her left hand began the breast stroke. "But you're always part of my dream threesome." It was a line and we both knew it, but at the moment, it didn't matter.

We had a twosome while Terry talked me through one of her threesome fantasies. Intense sex in a steamy hot tub after a night of heavy drinking left me more lightheaded than normal. Terry had to help me out of the tub, into the house, and into her bed since my wobbly legs were of no use to me. The smell of her wet, chlorinated hair was the last thing I remember before drifting off to sleep.

CHAPTER 32

The early morning sun peeked past the blinds on the windows and woke up Terry and me. Despite having to squint from the sunshine, I was surprised at how good I felt. Seeing our naked bodies intertwined had convalescing properties too.

"Morning." Terry turned away from the sun's prying rays.

"I can't believe how good I feel."

"Well." Terry looked at the clock. "We did get about eleven hours of sleep. That's probably twice what your body's used to getting."

"Oh, see, I was going to give credit to the wine," I joked.

"But not the hot tub or the hot sex?"

"That might have had a little to do with it." I kissed Terry on the cheek and streaked across the hall to wash up. My bedroom door was still closed, but I figured eleven hours of sleep for Franny or Kendra was just a nap. Terry and I were fully showered, clothed, and ready to take on the day when I went in to wake Franny and Kendra up.

"Hey guys." I pounced on the bed. "Whaddaya wanna do today?"

It took a solid ten minutes to get them to open their eyes, another ten to get them out of bed, and a half hour before they made their way upstairs to breakfast. We ate bagels and drank coffee out on the deck and decided to borrow Henry's car for a tour of the academy campus. Terry and Henry took Terry's car to Blockbuster Video and promised to have a week's worth of movies to watch by the time we got back from sightseeing.

I showed Franny and Kendra around the academy grounds and their mouths dropped open as they took in the sights. It helped me see the academy through their eyes, and their pride in me made me even prouder of what I had accomplished. I took them to the Academy Visitor's Center last so they could see all the photo montages there, the mock-up of a cadet room, and the gift shop. I wasn't surprised to see Franny filling up her basket with academy paraphernalia, but I was surprised to see Kendra doing the same.

"Oh wow." Franny stopped shopping as her eyes fixated on something in the distance.

I followed her gaze to realize she was madly in lust with one of my classmates. Pipes to be precise.

"He is hot. Are all the guys here that good looking?" Franny asked.

"Well, he's one of the uglier ones, but I'm sure he's got a great personality," I said.

"I want to meet him," Franny said.

"So go over and talk to him, you hussy," said Kendra.

"No, I can't. He looks so official in his uniform." Pipes had obeyed the rule that all fourth classmen were to be in uniform if they came on the academy grounds. I didn't feel like putting on my uniform and took the chance that I wouldn't see anyone who would recognize me.

"Shit, Franny, I'll do it." I walked toward Pipes, impressing Franny and Kendra.

"Excuse me, sir," I said in a girly-girl voice. "Could I get your autograph?"

Pipes turned around with a winning smile until he saw it was me and an even bigger, friendlier smile took over his face. He picked me up in a big bear hug while I motioned to Franny and Kendra to come over. I introduced them, and Pipes seemed very receptive to Franny's fawning.

"Hey, I'm having a big cookout at the house tonight. You guys need to come," Pipes said. I had forgotten that he lived in Colorado Springs. Franny would not have let me say no to the invite, so we got directions and promised to stop by later. I was trying to work a way to pawn Franny and Kendra off to Pipes's party so I could hang out alone with Terry, but the day wasn't unfolding that way.

CHAPTER 33

Franny had worked some magic and pulled Pipes's phone number out of him while we were at the gift shop, and she used generous hospitality as a ploy to call him later.

"Hi Daniel, it's Franny, Lexy's friend? Well, I just wanted to see what we could bring tonight. It was so nice of you to invite us. I don't want to come empty-handed."

Kendra yelled, "Why don't you bring condoms, huss? They'll come in handy when you come empty-handed." There was no way Pipes couldn't have heard the comment on his end.

"I'm sorry about my friend. She's just jealous. Good-looking men never pay attention to her." Franny continued her phone call with Pipes. They chatted for a while like they had been friends forever, and Pipes assured her that there was nothing she should bring but joked that condoms wouldn't be a bad idea. Franny had blushed at the comment, but you could tell that she wasn't going to show up empty-handed after all. I felt a little bragging would have been in order since I was the first of us to have used a condom with Pipes, but it wasn't the right time or crowd.

Franny, Kendra, and I went to the cookout. I had wanted Terry to go, too, but the academy's fraternization rules prohibited us from being seen together. We might have been able to pull off our combined presence somewhere else without anyone being the wiser, but Pipes and I were fourth-class cadets in Terry's squadron, and he would have recognized her and quickly deduced our situation.

I feigned a stomach pain to get the hell out of there and back to Terry, and the plot almost worked out better than I had planned. Franny didn't want to leave, and Pipes didn't want her to leave, either, and offered to drive her home later. That was the part that had worked out better than I had planned. Kendra decided she'd go back to Henry's with me since she didn't want to be Franny and Pipes's third wheel. That was the part that almost made it better than I had planned.

Terry's car was gone when Kendra and I pulled up to Henry's place and the lights were off inside. I was dreading alone time with Kendra, figuring she'd start the homosexual inquisition again. Our friendship had been perfect before that truth or dare kiss, before she revealed which way she felt I was oriented, before I let her into my head to suspect she was right, before her revelation thrust me into the crotch of another woman.

When we walked through the unlocked front door, Terry was putting a movie in the VCR.

"Perfect timing, you guys. Wanna watch *Halloween*?"

"Sure, why not?" I resigned myself to the fact that Kendra was going to be a part of this movie audience. I made myself comfortable on the couch next to Terry. Kendra didn't seem to have anything else planned and found a seat next to me. The room was pitch black, and under other circumstances, I would have made sure Terry didn't see any of the movie.

"Where's Henry?"

"She had a date. I don't think she'll be back tonight. Where's Franny?"

"She also had a date, and I don't think she'll be back tonight either," Kendra said.

"Yes, she will," I said. "It's not like they're gonna sleep together."

"Lexy, Franny is the one-night-stand queen," Kendra said, shocking me. She went on to tell me about Franny's rapid emergence as a slut back home.

I was in disbelief and began to feel protective of Pipes.

"So you really don't think she'll be calling for a ride tonight?" I asked Kendra.

"No. Is that Pipes guy a good guy?" Kendra probed.

"Piperata?" Terry asked.

"Yeah, Pipes is a good guy," I said.

"I have some classmates who want a piece of his pipe," Terry said.

"You included?" Kendra leaned forward to read Terry's face.

"Kendra, go grab some beer. I'm going to call Franny, then hit the little girl's room." I got up and gave Terry a sympathetic look.

Terry didn't look fazed by Kendra's insinuation.

I called Pipes's house, and he informed me that he was too drunk to drive Franny home. He put Franny on the phone, and when I offered to pick her up, she said tomorrow was fine. She had turned into quite the slut and so had Pipes.

When I got back from the bathroom, Terry and Kendra were sitting next to each other and Terry patted the area of the chaise lounge in front of her, "Sit here, babe."

I stared incredulously at Terry's slip.

"Lexy, it's okay. I told her. She already knew anyway. Let's stop pretending."

Kendra reassured me, "Lexy, sit down, let's watch the movie." She was the master of accepting everything and moving on as if nothing was different.

"Wh—what exactly did you say?" I stammered.

"Ken asked how long we'd been together, and I told her six months, that's all," Terry admitted.

A rush of confusing emotions flooded my head. I had been so worried about being alone with Kendra that I hadn't even considered the risks of leaving Terry and Kendra alone together. I was amazed that Terry was acknowledging a relationship with me and even more stunned that it had already been six months. I sat down in front of Terry between her legs. Terry hugged me and left her arms wrapped around me. Kendra grabbed a blanket from the back of the couch and threw it over all three of us. It felt as if the three of us had always watched movies together in the exact same seating arrangement.

I leaned forward, grabbed the remote, and pressed play to prevent any further conversation. The glow from the FBI's anti-piracy warning on the TV screen lit up Kendra's smile, and I threw a punch over my right shoulder. She returned the jab with an affectionate head butt, briefly leaning her head against my shoulder.

The story of Michael Myers wasn't in and of itself frightening, but watching it in the large living room without any lights helped my imagination create monsters out of shadows. I felt safe with Terry and Kendra so close. At one point when Jamie Lee Curtis was about to be attacked, all three of us were genuinely scared, and we all jumped in our seats. As we huddled together to prepare ourselves for the next knife-slashing surprise, Terry wrapped her right arm around Kendra, including her in our hug.

Kendra scooted closer and leaned into me, softly asking, "Am I squishing you, Lex?"

"No." I lost my focus on the movie. I was getting turned on. Kendra's hair smelled like berries, and Terry's left hand began to wander. I wondered what her right hand was up to. Kendra's moans gave me a rough idea that Terry's right hand was involved in similar wanderings.

Kendra rolled over, lying on her back with her head in my lap. She started to touch my breasts and before I could say anything, Terry pulled my mouth up to hers. Her kiss started out soft but gained momentum. Kendra rotated again and was on her right side, kissing my breasts through my shirt, while her hands found their way underneath. Kendra's hands were unexpectedly warm and gentle. Although I'd never given much thought to her sexual style, I would have guessed it to be rough and violent.

Terry continued our deep kiss while she led

my right hand with hers down to Kendra's crotch. Together, we rubbed her and I could feel the heat from Kendra's moans against my bare chest. She had worked my shirt up to expose my bra and her tongue's warmth melted my bra's silk as if it weren't even there. Terry's left hand unhooked my front bra clasp and held a tit out for Kendra's mouth. Kendra's tongue danced teasing circles while I forced Terry's hand into my jeans, where she was unencumbered by any underwear.

Terry leaned forward for better leverage and met Kendra's mouth. Over my right shoulder they kissed while Terry's strokes inside my wet jeans became more fervent. While Kendra and Terry's kiss intensified, I slid down and to the side and pushed Terry's shirt up and took her nipple in my mouth. I brought my hand back down to Kendra's crotch, where Terry was still rubbing her. I unbuttoned Kendra's pants and Terry and I slid Kendra's pants down far enough for Kendra to kick them off onto the floor.

We took a brief pause from whatever or whomever we were sucking or touching to re-choreograph our layout. Kendra used the break to pull off her panties. Terry and I both struggled for breath when we saw what the main attraction was now.

"Fuck Kendra," I gasped. Her pussy was completely hairless with a small gold stud protruding from her folds.

"That's hot," Terry said, moving toward Kendra to get a closer look and a closer lick.

"You wanna see it, Lex?" Kendra asked.

I did want to see it, but I hesitated. Terry put an encouraging hand against my back as she pushed me down toward Kendra's pierced clit. Kendra sat on the hassock with her legs spread wide open. I sat on the floor in front of her as Terry took a seat on the couch in front of Kendra. Terry's hands caressed my back as she gently pushed me forward into Kendra's open legs. Above me, I could hear the two of them kissing. A hand on the back of my head brought my mouth full onto Kendra's wet piercing. I hadn't realized that different women could have different tastes, but if it were a blind taste test, I would have known it wasn't Terry in my mouth.

Kendra's clit ring clicked against my teeth as I tried the alphabet on her with great success. Apparently, being eaten wasn't enough for Kendra though. She had an appetite of her own. She leaned forward, pushing me back as she kneeled on the couch. Terry had risen to a higher perch on the back of the couch, and Kendra's widespread knees were inside Terry's wider-spread feet. High above, I could hear Terry's groans as Kendra licked at her while I finished licking my ABCs on Kendra.

Kendra was the first to come, which I attributed to a failure to pace herself. After her orgasm, she collapsed to the side of the couch, taking up the full length of the chaise. I pivoted onto my knees and saw Terry's unpierced area right in front of me. Oblivious to Kendra's presence alongside us, I pulled Terry closer to my mouth and continued to work on my tongue's writing skills. She pulled her knees up tight to her body, allowing me to slide my fingers inside her. I could feel her orgasm approaching, but because I wasn't ready for it, I pulled my fingers out and retreated to teasingly licking the insides of her thighs.

"Oh, God, Lex, please finish," Terry cried. I continued to trace lines with my tongue from her knees down toward her pussy, coming playfully close to her clit and then licking up toward her opposite knee.

"Lexy, c'mon," Terry begged. I looked up and smiled back at her pitiful expression. Her hands had lost their strength and could not force my neck to bring my mouth to her closure. I could hear Kendra laughing. I looked over at Kendra, which only encouraged me to prolong Terry's orgasm. Kendra looked up at Terry, felt pity, and teamed up with her to get me back.

Having recuperated and regained more strength than I had left, Kendra picked me up like a professional wrestler and pulled me onto the chaise lounge. She held me on my back with one arm intertwined with mine and used her free hand to push Terry down to seek revenge on my thus-far neglected area.

Terry was familiar with getting me off and started right in on her tricks that drove me wild. I flung my right leg up over the chaise's arm rest and planted my left foot solidly on the floor. I brought my hips up to meet Terry's tongue while Kendra leaned over to suck my tits. I reached over my head and stroked Kendra's soft baldness. It was fantastic. I had my girlfriend eating me and my best friend sucking me. I wanted it to last forever.

Terry thrust her fingers into me and started the rhythmic in and out that complemented her circular licks, a deadly combination that had a hundred percent success rate. I slid two fingers into Kendra, which she rode up and down.

"I'm coming T, I'm coming," I shouted.

"No you're not," Terry said, deliberately pulling her mouth away and her fingers out. The sudden absence ached.

"Finish her Terry," Kendra said, still riding my hand and getting wetter with each up and down. Kendra panted with frustration as she tried to get Terry to finish what she had started. Terry conceded only halfway by resuming her finger strokes. Kendra, on the verge of her second orgasm, took matters into her own mouth by stretching out and sucking my clit.

Kendra's tongue was cooler than Terry's and her motions were different and new. My fingers were still inside Kendra and Terry's were still inside me. The position change and the erotica of my first threesome pushed me over the edge. As I came, my pussy closed down on Terry's fingers and my body went limp. Terry's fingers waited inside for a moment, then danced me into a second orgasm. All three of us recovered slowly, lying there in a new blend of our musky scents.

Kendra was the first one up and headed to the downstairs bathroom to take a shower. Terry and I went into Henry's bathroom and stepped into the large shower together.

"Was that close to what you dreamt about?" I asked, pressing my body up against hers.

"Better."

"I don't recall you actually finishing."

"It doesn't matter, that was fucking hot."

As I soaped up Terry's back, I reached between her legs and held her tightly with one arm as she braced herself against the shower's walls while I stroked her into completion. She laid her head back onto my shoulder and took a deep breath as she rubbed the back of my neck.

CHAPTER 34

The rest of spring break was more fun than Terry or I had planned. Neither Kendra nor Terry nor I talked about our movie night, but it was a definite bonding experience for the three of us. Franny spent more time at Pipes's place than at Henry's, but that worked out for the best as officially coming out to and with Kendra was enough for me for one week.

On Friday morning, Franny was busy packing her suitcases and talking on the phone to Pipes. Kendra pulled me out of the room and into Terry's. Terry was sitting on the bed reading, and I hopped on the bed next to her while Kendra shut and locked the door.

"I just wanted to say goodbye and that I had a lot of fun." Kendra crawled onto the bed with us.

"It was a dream come true," Terry said, meaning it literally.

"I am happy for you, Lexy."

"Shut up, Kendra, you're just happy you were right."

"Honestly, doll, it was never about that. I just wanted you to be happy and to be comfortable with it. I've known for a long time. It was killing me when you were so pissed off at me. I hated not talking to you every day."

"Me too." I reached across the bed and hugged Kendra, sad that she was leaving, happy that we had shared something so intimate.

"And Terry, you take care of my girl. You are a fuckin' hottie, but if you break my girl's heart, I'll have to kick your ass."

"Deal." Terry hugged Kendra too.

Kendra leaned out of Terry's hug and kissed me on the lips. I kissed her back until Terry pulled Kendra to her and demanded the same type of kiss. The three of us exchanged deep, open-mouthed, tongue-inserting kisses until we heard Franny closing her conversation with Pipes.

"Great, get me all turned on and put me on a plane with Franny," Kendra chided.

After one more round of kisses for the road, Terry and I drove Franny and Kendra to the airport and watched them from the car as they walked into the terminal.

"Well, that was an interesting week," I confessed.

"So is Kendra gay?" Terry asked. A fair question based on her performance this week.

"Kendra would fuck a mop handle just to make household chores more interesting," I said.

"Well, I'll take your word on that," Terry laughed, "but, I don't think the week could have gone any better."

"Yeah, except now I'm all horny again, and we're at an airport."

"Well, let's get the hell out of here and find a nice detour on the way home."

We ran to the parking lot and sped away but failed to find any place suitable for car sex along the drive back to Henry's. Unfulfilled sexual desire distorted rational thought and when Terry pulled into Patty's Pleasure Palace—Sex, Toys, and Videos, I was a willing shopper.

We rushed through the store, in part because we wanted to get out of there as soon as possible and in part because we wanted to get into each other as soon as possible. I wasn't positive of Terry's purchases, but it was shiny and needed batteries. We had made it in and out of the store in record time. Then again, any time would have been a record for me since that was my first sex toy store shopping experience.

Still horny and still not thinking straight, so to speak, Terry drove us to a seedy motel that charged by the hour. We parked the car two blocks away, she ran in to get a room, and I followed her into our love suite that was ours, all ours, for the next sixty minutes.

"Can you believe this dump?" She laughed as we barged through the plywood door.

The room was cinnamon-red and pink, a putrid combination of colors sure to dry up even the most perverse of sex offenders. But not us. We were horny college kids with sixty minutes to kill and a sleek vibrator with which to kill them.

CHAPTER 35

"What the hell are we supposed to do with that?" I raised my voice to be heard over the buzz of the silver bullet.

"Lay back, I'll show you." Terry pushed me back onto the Pepto-Bismol pink bedspread and stripped off my clothes, then hers. She laid the humming pole up against my mound and it took less than an instant for numbing tingles to surge through my body.

"Wow," was all I could say.

Terry straddled me and the vibrator, sliding back and forth as it hummed its tune between us. It was exciting to be in the sleazy, hourly rate motel using a vibrator with such a sexually confident woman. In the past week, she had taken me to new places in my sex life. Hell, in the past six months, she had given me a sex life. I stared up at her as she rode me and the battery-powered pulses. I wasn't in the mood for gentle sex, which worked out well since our current environment didn't lend itself to gentle sex.

I seesawed myself up, pushing her off of me and onto her back. I grabbed the vibrator, forced Terry's legs open, and teased her with the tip. Terry didn't need foreplay and covered my hand with hers and pushed the vibrator deep inside her. Her body muffled the noise, but I could still feel the pulsations against the palm of my hand.

Terry's head hung upside down off the edge of the bed, which *Cosmopolitan* magazine assured me intensified any orgasm. I was excited to test the theory, but the race for time was between our hourly investment and Terry losing consciousness from a flood of blood to her head. I used the wand like a magician, making it appear and disappear in and out of her. Terry's stomach was starting to ripple with her impending climax and she bent her knees to let me get deeper. She began to slide off the bed as her bent legs shifted her fulcrum away from me. I held her legs as tight as I could, speeding up my thrusts in the hopes that she would come before she crashed.

"Fuck me faster Lex!"

I did.

"Fuck me deeper Lex!"

I did.

I saw a black dial on the back of the vibrator and used my palm to turn it to the left. The pressure from my palm pushed the bullet deeper into Terry and at the same time caused it to increase its pace of pulsation. That was enough to push her over the edge, literally.

Terry went crashing to the floor, taking me and the silver baton with her. Any remorse I felt in being the primary party responsible for her falling off the bed was replaced by gratification in being the primary party responsible for her dramatic orgasm.

"Oh God, Lex, to the moon!" Terry hollered as she started her descent off the bed. I wasn't sure what she meant. I never asked and she never explained. But I took her phrase as a good sign, especially when it was followed by, "Whooooeeeee!"

We were crumpled on the floor with the buzzing bullet still sticking out of Terry, sending more jolts of spasms through her body. I pulled Terry to her feet and the bullet buzzed its way out of her. We laughed together as we watched the vibrator drone around on the shag carpet, wiggling like a fish out of water.

"Let's get out of here," I suggested.

"Hey, we still have thirty minutes left."

"I'll make it up to you at Henry's."

"I'll take you up on that," Terry smiled.

We ran back to Terry's car and raced back to Henry's, leaving our battery-powered toy in the seedy room of the sleazy, hourly rate motel.

CHAPTER 36

Going back to the Zoo was a relative lull compared to my mind-blowing week of sexual adventure with Terry. Seeing Terry in the squadron halls without being able to smile at, talk to, or mount her was both frustrating and titillating. Sexual tension built to near combustion during the week, finally to be released on weekend sexathons. But as we got closer to recognition, I had no idea that I would have to go cold Terry for more than a month.

"SMACKs! Get your asses out here," said the ubiquitous voice from the hallway.

Like obedient disciples, we scurried out into the hallway and lined up shoulder to shoulder in front of the upper-class mouthpiece.

"Recognition is around the corner, but you guys are far from earning the right to be recognized. From now on, all passes are revoked. You have all been assigned hell masters, but it will be up to the hell master to make contact with you. There will be no hazing and no after-hours hell master missions. If you are hazed or instructed to accomplish an after-hours mission, you will immediately inform the squadron commander. Is this clear?"

"Yes sir!" we all voiced in unison. His comments about hazing were required by the academy officer staff. What he was really saying, though, was that there would be hazing and after-hours missions. If we had the balls to rat out our hell master, it would be our word against theirs. And they would deny it until the cows came home.

Hell masters were three degrees who had the memories from last year's recognition most recent on their minds. They got together and selected a four-degree hell child who would be their slave up until hell week, the week that led up to recognition. More motivated upperclassmen usually joined in on the fun and picked on either the sharp SMACKs or the severely incompetent ones. The date of recognition, and therefore the start of hell week, was a closely guarded secret. Traditionally, it was somewhere between spring break and graduation, so we were prime targets for asinine requests and a resulting lack of sleep.

"Eerie Cat, get over here," Cadet Teason hollered at me from down the hall.

I sprinted to her only to smell the strong scent of multiple whiskey sours on her breath, an obvious result of the short walking commute to and from the cadet sports bar.

"You will be my alarm clock until recognition, do you understand?" she slurred.

"Yes ma'am," I said at a normal volume since it was during the academic call to quarters.

"You will come into my room starting at zero five forty-five and wake me up quietly. If I hit you on top of the head," she demonstrated with a gentle tousle of my hair, "you will consider that the snooze button and come back in five minutes, got that?"

"Yes ma'am."

"Good. Carry on." With that, I went back about my business.

Knowing that Cadet Terry Teason had trouble waking up in the morning was a fact that most fourth classmen, and perhaps most of her own classmates, did not know. Nonetheless, I set my alarm for earlier than normal for my first day as a human alarm clock, anticipating a series of snooze buttons. However, my actual wake-up wasn't a result of the alarm I had set.

What woke me up was the trifecta of the pungent smell of rubbing alcohol, the orange flames coming from our sink's countertop, and the "WOOOF!" that announced the ignition of the alcohol. By the time

Paige and I figured out that all was not normal in our room, the flames had dwindled to small flickers as the supply of alcohol burned up. Although my heart was already beating at its target heart rate, it picked up a few beats per minute when we flicked the room lights on and saw two headless human figures floating by our closet. In actuality, the apparitions were our bathrobes stuffed with newspaper, hanging on their hangers. They had to have been taken during the day because I hadn't even noticed that mine was missing and wouldn't have noticed until I needed it when I went to the showers in the morning.

"What the hell?" I started.

"Oh, how cool! It must be from our hell masters." Paige was ever the morning person even at three thirty a.m. "Look!" The early hours did not hamper Paige's observational skills as she quickly noticed a note pinned to one of the robes.

"Seivers and Erecat, I have chosen you both because you have impressed me, and I want you to finish off your four-degree year with pride and honor. If you choose to accept the challenges of hell week, retrieve the squadron commander's toothbrush and tape it to the backside of the third-stall toilet in the squadron men's room by 2200 this Friday."

The thrill of the challenge and the benefit of an accomplice woke me up in time to see the wheels in

Paige's head turning as she began to plot our strategy. We had our plan finalized within an hour, and I had enough time for a half-hour nap before I had to start getting myself ready to play alarm clock for Terry.

"Why are you getting up already?" Paige asked.

"Teason requested me as her alarm clock. I have to wake her up at zero five forty-five and every five minutes thereafter until she decides to roll out of bed," I explained.

"How fun! I hope I get additional duties too!"

I rolled my eyes as I headed off to the showers. I changed in the bathroom to avoid waking up Paige a second time and, with wet hair, headed toward Terry's room. I knocked lightly, entered the room, and quietly climbed a couple steps on the ladder leading up to Terry's bed.

"Cadet Teason, the time is five forty-five. I am here to wake you up," I whispered.

Terry rolled over in her bunk, smiled sleepily at me, then ran her fingers through my hair. I took that as a snooze request and climbed back down the steps and left her room. After five minutes of studying the newspaper for my three current events articles, I went back and repeated the routine. It took four iterations to wake Terry up, and by the time she decided to obey her alarm clock, the halls were alive with sleepy upperclassmen trudging to the showers to start their days.

Waking up Terry proved to be the easier task leading up to recognition. Now and again, she gave me some mornings off, but since I wasn't able to be in bed with her at Henry's, it was at least nice to see her in bed at school. Paige and I went above and beyond our hell master's call to duty in regard to the toothbrush tasker. At ten p.m. on Friday, our hell master should have walked into the third stall to retrieve the toothbrush but instead saw our squadron commander's stuffed robe, sitting on the toilet, reading a newspaper whose headline read, "Bring it on!" And of course, sticking out of the mouth of the papier-mâché head was the squadron commander's toothbrush.

CHAPTER 37

Getting into the men's room Friday night was easy. While the fourth classmen were confined to the academy proper, the upperclassmen gladly escaped the grounds at the end of classes on Friday afternoon.

Paige and I were still giddy from sneaking the papier-mâché figure into the bathroom, with Pipes's help, when someone knocked on our door. We naturally assumed we had been caught in the men's room with the squadron commander's toothbrush and his bathrobe.

"Enter please, sir or ma'am," we said the requisite phrase in unison.

The door opened, Cadet Teason popped her head in. "Reset my alarm for zero eight hundred tomorrow, Eerie Cat."

"Yes ma'am," I said.

"You have to do it on the weekend too?" Paige asked after Cadet Teason had left. She echoed my confusion that I would have alarm clock duties on the weekend and probably didn't pick up on my surprise that Terry would even be on campus over the weekend.

"Guess so," was all I said.

"You know, she would have been my guess for your answer back in Jack's Valley," Paige said.

The disorientation regarding my weekend wake-up responsibilities was compounded by Paige's left-field statement. It quickly came back that she was referring to her brief query of, "If you could hook up with any upperclassman, who would it be?" as well as her follow-on, "It can be male or female."

"Let's go ask Pipes to check if the dummy's still on the toilet." I just wanted to get Paige's mind off of Terry. My mind could use the distraction, too, because all I could think about was a more erotic way of waking Terry up in ten hours.

CHAPTER 38

At eight a.m. Saturday, I knocked lightly on Cadet Teason's door and then let myself in her room. As I tried to shut the door quietly behind me to avoid waking up her roommate, I heard Terry's voice, "Lock the door behind you."

I looked up to her roommate's bed, inspection ready with hospital corners and perfect folds in the comforter and realized we were alone in her room. I climbed up the steps to Terry's bed like I had for the past week. As I reached my pinnacle, Terry threw back her covers to show off the pajamas her parents had given her twenty-one years earlier. Instinctively, I looked to make sure I had locked the door because there would be absolutely no way to explain what I was about to do to Terry if anyone were to walk in.

I finished the ascent to her bed, straddled her as I crawled down her body and began to lick her snooze button. Although somewhat muffled by her legs, my ears did pick up a surprised inhale coming from Terry. I wasted no time at the buffet Terry had laid before me while she pushed a finger's width of my gym shorts aside to make way for her tongue. I lapped at her crotch while she rocked mine against her mouth, guiding my hips back and forth with her hands. We tried to keep as quiet as possible, not because we cared about waking anyone up, but because we were breaking a multitude of rules.

Terry quickly gave up on the task of licking me into submission and just took the licking I was giving her. She brought her hips up harder and farther as I felt her pre-orgasm quivers against my tongue. Recognizing the ceiling's bracing properties, Terry shifted her feet skyward. As she came, she dug her nails into my hips and stucco from the ceiling rained down into my hair. The most noise from our brief encounter came when Terry's feet dropped loudly to the mattress. I spun around and kissed my way up to her breasts.

"Should I come back in five minutes?" I asked.

"How 'bout you come now," she said as she rolled me under her warm, moist, naked body.

"Terry, are you sure we should—" she took the rest of my sentence away when she forced my shorts aside and slid two fingers into me.

"I love fucking you," she moaned into my ear as she drifted in and out of me. I spread my legs farther for her, bracing myself with one leg on the ceiling and one against the wall. I reached down and stroked circles around her clit and the bed unit rocked more violently, knocking a few of her textbooks from their upright position.

"I can't wait until you and I can fuck whenever we want to," Terry growled as her second orgasm approached.

Now, I'm not proud of seeing an exploitation opportunity, but at that moment, I figured all was fair in sex and war. I was having sex with Terry and SMACKs were at war with the upperclassmen. "When will that be?" I asked, wondering if Terry was not of sound mind enough to reveal the date of recognition.

"Lex, you know I can't tell you that," Terry said, as she kept sliding in and out of me and rode the quickening circles I was tracing on her.

"That's too bad," I said, as I withdrew and stopped my massage and clinched my legs together to stop hers.

"Oh, come on Lexy, that's not fair. Please, let me finish."

"Say the magic date."

"Fourteen May," she caved.

"See, that wasn't so bad," I said as I gave her hand room to move and slipped my fingers inside her. I propped my hips up higher, which pushed my fingers deeper into her. Like clockwork, the thrill of our taboo tryst awoke our well-timed orgasms.

CHAPTER 39

"I know when recognition is going to be," I panted, out of breath for a number of reasons, only willing to admit a couple of them to Paige.

"When? How'd you find out? Where have you been? You've been gone for like twenty-five minutes." Paige fired her questions at me.

"Fourteen May." I thought it best to avoid the other questions because I was a shitty liar, and the truth wasn't something I wanted to reveal to Paige.

"But how did you find out?"

"I was coming back from waking up Cadet Teason and some three degrees were talking about it. They had their backs to me, and I ducked behind the Cadet in Charge of Quarters desk and eavesdropped." Apparently, I was a better liar than I gave myself credit for.

"I can't believe they didn't see you, and I can't believe you know when recognition's gonna be." Paige squealed. "How long did you have to wait behind the desk? What if one of them saw you? Was your heart just pounding out of your chest?"

"Paige, focus. We know the date now, and since it's only two weeks away, we can go all out for our hell master."

"Good point," Paige said, satisfied that how I found out wasn't as important as what I found out.

Knowing when recognition was made life a little easier, if only for the fact that we knew specifically when our hell would end. The real hell would be the week immediately before recognition. That's when all the stops would be pulled out and upperclassmen got their last digs in us before treating us as quasi peers. Paige and I surpassed every task our hell master threw at us. Our stellar performance as hell children helped reduce any additional requests from other upperclassmen seeking last-minute power trips.

CHAPTER 40

The week leading up to recognition had been physically and emotionally trying. We fought to salvage the last bits of energy into useful acts of fourth-class exploits. Adrenaline was at an all-time high as the thirty-two of us gathered in Lucky's room, making last minute adjustments to our service dress coats.

"Can you believe we made it?" Paige adjusted the clasp on the back of my nametag. This required her to reach into my service coat and brought the back of her hand against my chest. Paige's touch did nothing for me, but I quickly catalogued the move as a crafty way of making a subtle pass in the future.

"No. It's been fun though, hasn't it?" I said.

"I couldn't have done it without you, you know." Paige's emotion welled up in her eyes.

"You either. You've helped make it fun. Thanks." I meant my words. Our hug was a heartfelt thank you to one another.

Our Hallmark moment was interrupted by Cadet Tollet barging into the room unannounced by a knock. We all knocked into each other in an effort to snap to attention in the presence of the upperclassman.

"Hey guys, relax. I just want to let you know how this is gonna work." Cadet Tollet talked to us as if we were human. "When we get done here, I want you to gather out in the hallway in front of Lucky's room." Hearing Cadet Tollet call Lucky "Lucky" sounded so foreign from the mouth that usually called us by names like "Shit Head" or "Fuck Up."

"I will be at the Cadet in Charge of Quarters desk and will call you one by one. When you hear your name, I want you to walk with purpose down the middle of the hallway to the desk, square your corner as you turn left, walk down to the other end of the hall, about-face, and form up together. Do you understand?"

"Yes sir," we said in unison.

"Good. Now you guys walk proudly. You've busted your ass this past year and you've earned this. As you walk down the hallways, walk tall and remember how you all met last June as scared kids and have spent the past eleven months growing into a professional team. I've been proud to train you guys this past year, and I'll be proud watching each of you walk down these halls at attention for the last time."

Cadet Tollet had been our primary trainer, the first to chew our asses out when we screwed up and the first to cheer us on when we needed that last bit of motivation to accomplish whatever task was at hand. We had hated him and loved him, sometimes at the same moment. He had made us better and we knew it. We watched in silence as he walked out of Lucky's room. We filed out slowly, patting each other on the shoulders for jobs well done. Everything leading up to this moment was designed to differentiate us from regular college kids, to prepare us for a future much different from theirs. Outsiders could never fully understand or appreciate how these experiences bonded us as brothers and sisters for life.

"Richard Booker Anderson." Cadet Tollet's voice boomed down an otherwise silent hallway. Book, as we knew him, pulled the tails of his service coat down, straightened up into a tall soldier, and marched purposefully down the hallway. We watched him stop in front of Cadet Tollet and render a crisp salute, which Cadet Tollet respectfully returned before Book left faced and disappeared down the other part of the L-shaped hallway out of our sight. It was the first time we had watched a classmate stray from the group without an ensuing scream fest about the importance of teamwork and support for our classmates. When Lucky's name was called, he smiled a big grin at us before he marched down the hall and saluted Cadet Tollet, just as Book had. He too disappeared out of sight.

Even though common sense and a rudimentary understanding of military procedure would have predicted we were being called out alphabetically, I was still at the back of the pack when the "E" last names came up. My heart raced as Cadet Tollet called out my name. My classmates patted me on the back as they made a small path for me to get to my starting point. With my eyes firmly fixed on Cadet Tollet, I put one foot in front of the other, until I was face to face with him. As I snapped my sharpest salute, I said a quiet, "Thank you, Cadet Tollet."

"Congrats, Lex." I was amazed that Cadet Tollet knew my nickname and had actually called me by it. But what took my breath away was the sight before me as I did my left face to start the last half of my recognition walk. The fluorescent light tubes had all been unseated to darken the hallway. What lit the hallway instead was a candle held in the hand of each squadron upperclassman, standing along either side of the hallway, also wearing their service dress. I didn't think I could extend my back any straighter nor throw my shoulders back any farther, but with a deep inhale, I stood taller and prouder.

As I slowly walked by the upperclassmen, who had been the enemy for the past eleven months, they whispered things like, "Good job, Lex," or "Well done, Alexis." I stopped trying to contain the smile that took over my face as I strode toward the small formation of my classmates at the end of the hallway. When I got to them, I spun myself 180 degrees and found my spot in the ranks as Cadet Tollet continued to call the rest of the names. Watching my classmates, my friends, make that left turn and see the supportive upperclassmen was almost as gratifying as when I did it.

When all the names had been called and the last fourth classman had joined the formation, we stood in five columns, six or seven deep. Cadet Hartgrove, our squadron commander, a firstie just weeks from becoming a second lieutenant, marched to a spot in front of us.

"Eleven months ago, the thirty-two of you entered the academy as basic cadets. Ten months ago, the thirty-two of you became fourth classmen in cadet squadron thirty-two. Today, the thirty-two of you are recognized for your perseverance and teamwork." In talking with my other classmates, not every squadron had a zero percent attrition rate. Many squadrons lost fourth-class cadets as they quit or were kicked out for academic violations or behavioral infringements. As the list of infractions Terry and I had committed infiltrated my mind, I realized how lucky I was to be standing where I was.

As Cadet Hartgrove spoke, the upperclassmen who lined the halls formed up behind him, the collective glow of their candles creating an enormous halo behind him.

"I know this wasn't an easy year, but if it was easy, everyone could do it. Not everyone can do what you've done. Be proud of that. Be proud that the hardest year is behind you, but know that the years ahead of you won't be easy either. But for now, celebrate this success. You are dismissed."

At the word "dismissed," we simultaneously did the dismissal movement, which entailed an about-face then one step forward to break up the organized formation. Meanwhile, the hall darkened as the upperclassmen blew out their candles. As we turned back toward our upperclassmen, they were coming at us with smiling faces and extended hands. People started replacing the fluorescent tubes and restoring light to the now-smoky hallway.

CHAPTER 41

"Everyone, down to the SAR," shouted someone, directing us to the squadron assembly room. For the first time since we arrived at the academy almost a year prior, we were walking like normal human beings. We weren't squaring corners. We weren't greeting every upperclassman with a loud salutation. We walked down to the room engaging in mindless chatter, not because we had anything to say, but just because we could. Most of the upperclassmen beat us down there, and the three degrees were lined up in front of the rest of the two degrees and firsties. Like a gaggle of girls at a coed dance, we clumped together across from the three degrees.

Cadet Third Class Ellesandro stepped forward from the line and called, "Book."

Book walked up to Cadet Ellesandro, who then pinned a one-inch pair of silver prop and wings on Book's service coat lapel. The prop and wings symbolized our status as upperclassmen. As recognized SMACKs, we were now authorized to wear the prop and wings on our flight cap like the three academy upperclassmen. As Cadet Ellesandro stepped back into line, Book blended back into our rapidly organizing group. One by one, this time by our first names or nicknames, we were called forward by a three degree. When Cadet Third Class Woodard called out, "Lex and Paige," we realized that the three degrees were, for the first time, identifying themselves to their hell children.

"I had a lot of fun being your hell master," Cadet Woodard started. "You guys went above and beyond what I expected and asked. Thanks for making hell week a challenge for me." He winked as he pinned my prop and wings insignia on my lapel.

"Thank you sir," I said.

"Lex, my name's Randy, not sir anymore," he corrected me.

"Okay, Randy." I heard Paige giggle as she heard me call him Randy to his face, because we had always called the upperclassmen by their first names when we were among other SMACKs.

When all of us had shiny new prop and wings on our lapels, we congratulated each other as the upperclassmen merged into our celebration. Cadet Hartgrove, or Tim, came up to me and pinned another pair of prop and wings on my lapel and congratulated me. After him, another firstie pinned a pair on me, then a two degree, then another firstie. Within minutes, I looked down at my lapel to see thirteen pairs of prop and wings pinned randomly on my lapels. I glanced at my classmates, who had varying numbers of prop and wings on their lapels as well. Some had only a few pairs, others were maxed out on fabric space like I was. It was obvious that nothing obligated the upperclassmen beyond our hell masters to give us a pair of prop and wings, so I took it as an honor to get the additional pins.

"Congrats, Lexy." Terry approached me and shook my hand.

"Thanks." I waited for her to pin me. The smile that I had worn since upstairs in the squadron faded as Terry went on to congratulate my other classmates. The sting inflicted from her not pinning a pair of prop and wings on me was deepened when I watched her pin Lucky and Pipes.

I was in no position to demand her respect for what I had accomplished alongside my classmates, but I expected her to understand the hidden complexity of my accomplishment. She knew how difficult it was to be a SMACK, and she knew how difficult it was to be gay at the academy. I was pissed that she didn't recognize and reward my successful completion of my first year as a gay SMACK.

Fuck her. I knew I had accomplished something bigger than I ever thought possible, and I was proud of myself for having done it while figuring out how to do it as a gay fourth-class cadet. I was proud of myself. I was comfortable with myself. At that instant, I felt the need to prove that I didn't need Terry or her acceptance. I had three more years at the academy, and the lessons I learned in my first year as a gay cadet would help me explore my options with other women during the next three.

Mandy was the first other woman who came to mind. We had endured the same challenge of the fourth-class year. We had a special connection. And I knew she was the one person I could be seen with that would drive Terry mad. I made it a point to find her as soon as I could change into civilian clothes and track her down. I hoped it would hurt Terry as much to see Mandy and me together as she had just hurt me.

CHAPTER 42

"Man, wasn't that awesome?" Paige asked as we got back to our room. We were both unbuttoning our service coats before the door was completely closed. The last time we wore civilian clothes on the academy campus was eleven months ago when we first checked in. We both had a hidden stash of civilian clothes, and we wasted no time getting into them. I chose a pair of jeans, recently purchased, that fit a little more snugly than the pants I normally wore. Comfort be damned, I was out to impress Mandy only because I was out to make Terry jealous. Besides, with the series of unfinished trysts Mandy and I had started, I didn't plan on being in the jeans for long.

"Isn't it a little late, or early, for Christmas?" Paige popped out from behind her bed unit wearing tight black capris and a snug, frilly, flowered blouse. I followed her eyes to my desk and saw the small box I had seen on top of Terry's backpack back in January when we had returned from Christmas break. For obvious reasons, the gift tag announcing the gift giver was absent. The same flood of nausea that had hit me then, hit me again. Walking in on Mandy and me had prevented Terry from giving me the gift back in January. Now, five months later, I was using Mandy to get back at Terry.

I felt the pit in my stomach that always accompanied the realization that I had overreacted. Using Mandy as a solution to my jumped conclusion wouldn't have been productive for me and Mandy any more so than it would have been for me and Terry. Fortunately, I had not acted on my scheming plan of vengeance.

"What is it?" Paige pestered over my shoulder.

I was tentative to open the box in front of Paige but did so anyway. My uncertainty grew as I saw the ring box inside the wrapped cardboard box.

"Is it from Cadet Teason?" Paige asked.

My attention shifted from the box in my hand to Paige. "Why would you say that?" I asked, incredulous that she would link Terry and me together as well as have the balls to confront me about it so nonchalantly.

"Well, I figured you two were an item, and now that we're technically upperclassmen, maybe she's giving you a ring to seal the relationship."

I said nothing because I couldn't talk.

"Lex, it's no big deal," Paige said.

"But, how?" was all I could get out.

"Lex, I'm not an idiot. I pick up on more than I let on. If she's who makes you happy, then I'm happy for you. Now open the box."

Listening to Paige was like listening to Kendra right before I left for the academy. I cursed my luck of attracting hyper-perceptive friends but welcomed the fact that the two insightful people in my life were understanding friends.

I opened the box to see a pair of prop and wings nested in the box's velvet lips. Paige's sigh of disappointment went for both of us.

Paige's upbeat personality revived itself as she kissed me on the cheek and said, "Push for the ring," then skipped out the door. Paige and Terry collided at the room's threshold and after Paige excused herself, she winked at me over Terry's shoulder.

"I see you got my gift," Terry shut the door behind her. "Congrats, Lex. I knew you could do it. I had confidence in you."

"Since Christmas, I suppose." I held up the flattened wrapping paper adorned with Santa and Rudolph.

"Well, I was gonna give you the prop and wings after Christmas break as a symbolic motivator to get you through to recognition, but—"

"Yeah, sorry about that." I remembered Terry's surprise intrusion on Mandy and me.

"OBE." Terry referred to the military acronym that stood for Overcome By Events.

"Why didn't you pin these on me downstairs with everyone else?" I asked.

"I didn't want it to be too obvious that we were dating."

"Are we dating?"

"Well, that's why I'm here. I came to ask you out." Terry stopped long enough to read my confused look. "I mean on a real date. Dinner and a movie kind of thing."

I was confused. Being with Terry was comfortable. Well, sex with Terry was comfortable. Reflecting back, we'd never really had much in the way of conversation, but that had served us both just fine. So, there seemed no better way to use my free weekend pass than to spend it with Terry.

"Oh, well, yes." I smiled.

"Good. I'm glad you said yes, because I already signed us both out. Come get me whenever you're ready to go."

"I'm ready now," I told her.

This brought a smile to her face, and I followed my girlfriend out of my room.

As we sauntered down the hallway, Mandy rounded the corner, crossing the previously impervious boundary between her squadron and mine. Her smile fell when she saw Terry and me. My heart sank, partly because I saw the pain in her face, partly because I hadn't gotten the chance to congratulate her on her accomplishment of recognition, and partly because I owed her a conversation to come to some sort of resolution on "us." We'd had a couple interrupted and unfinished starts to something we never had the chance to define, and there was an unspoken need to figure out what that was. The hallway with my current companion didn't facilitate that conversation.

"Hey, Roberts." Terry's salutation overpowered my greeting that used Mandy's first name.

Terry's belittling use of Mandy's last name when she knew her first name was a typical verbal power play that Mandy and I picked up on.

Mandy played her game with sportsmanship. "Hi, Cadet Teason."

It made me sick to my stomach to see Terry treat Mandy this way solely because she thought whatever she thought about Mandy and me. I didn't know Mandy well enough to how she took this, but Terry's little stunt was not lost on either of us.

"I'll catch ya later, Mandy," I said, as Terry corralled me to the stairwell to start the descent to the cadet parking lot.

CHAPTER 43

Terry drove us down to Beau Jo's pizza, where she ordered us a mountain pie on thick honey-white crust. It was like a real date. It was awkward. I was nervous, and we could find nothing to talk about.

"Why are you so quiet?" I broke the silence of our staring contest as we endured our pizza's long, slow arrival to our table.

"I'm not sure," Terry said.

"So, what movie are we going to go see?" I tapped my fingers nervously on the table, probably saying more in Morse code than I was with my mouth.

"I hadn't really thought about it," Terry said.

I was out of poor conversation starters, and Terry had none to break the unnatural silence growing more deafening with each passing minute.

The pizza finally arrived at our table, and we both pawed at it, grateful for something to excuse our lack of conversation. In reflecting on our previous conversations, I realized the really climactic ones had been nonverbal.

"You know, I really don't know that much about you." I admitted the realization that came during our silent consumption of two pieces of pizza.

"Nor I you."

I propped my elbow on the table, narrowed my eyes, and leaned in like Larry King on an interview and said, "So tell me about yourself."

Terry either didn't catch that I was kidding or didn't think it was funny. She began a mechanical rendition of what would never be a best-selling autobiography. I sat uneasily as I listened to the dull, monotone monster I had birthed. When she had finished, she matter-of-factly said, "Now, you."

I tried to bring some levity back to the table by leaning back in my chair, crossing my arms across my chest, and flippantly replying, "Well Terry, I'm a test tube baby raised in a genetic research laboratory, and I've never met my parents, but based on my perfect SAT scores I'd have to say they were first-class geniuses. Although I turned down full scholarships to Harvard, Yale, and the Sally Struthers home education program for TV and VCR repair, I came to the academy to meet women."

I stopped before going any further because Terry's face revealed a clear misunderstanding of what it was I was trying to do.

"Terry, I was just trying to be funny. Dates are supposed to be fun and full of lively, entertaining conversation," I tried to explain.

"Oh," was the witty retort from the master conversationalist. It was painful how difficult this seemed to be. In addition to feeling embarrassed for Terry, I was taken aback by my unsubstantiated infatuation with the boring person sitting across from me. I thought I liked this woman, but I realized I only liked sex with this woman. I was looking forward to being at the movies, where we were encouraged not to talk.

We survived the rest of the meal in silence and made it to the movies in time to walk into a dark theater already showing previews. Another awkward stretch of silence avoided.

When the lights dimmed further to announce the beginning of the main attraction, Terry's hand began to caress my thigh. Before the opening credits were through, her hand had found a comfortable place and rhythm in between my legs. I was so distracted that it took several minutes to realize that Terry's idea of a real date was pizza, no conversation, and a movie turned pornographic by her poor spectator skills. The date was shaping up to be disappointing on many levels, except one, so I slid down in my chair, propped my feet up on the seat in front of me and let

Terry do what Terry did best: me. Sex with Terry was comforting in that it was familiar. But even though I had no complaints about our physical chemistry, the realization hit me that we had no other chemistry between us.

I knew right then great sex with Terry wasn't going to be enough to satisfy my desire to experience more of the lesbian life. I wanted to flirt with women and feel that magic connection when you both realize there are mutual feelings of attraction. I wanted to date women and feel that nervous first-date giddiness. I wanted to be on dates that ended too quickly and left me wanting more. I still wanted to have sex, but I knew I wanted more than just sex.

CHAPTER 44

"Wasn't that better than talking?" Terry asked once we got back in her car.

Not really.

"You wanna go to Henry's and hang out?" Terry asked.

"Actually, I think I'd rather go back to school. Would you mind dropping me off?"

"You have to be kidding."

I actually couldn't believe I was requesting to be back at the Zoo rather than with Terry. "Well, I'm not. I'd like to call my parents and tell them about recognition. Do you mind driving me back up there?"

"You can call them from Henry's place." Terry started driving toward Henry's.

"Terry, please take me back to the Zoo." It felt odd ordering an upperclassman to do something, but Terry made me feel trapped.

"Are you breaking up with me?" Terry asked with an incredulous tone.

"Are we going out?" I replied with the same tone.

"Lex, we just went on a date."

"Terry, we ate pizza in silence and had sex in a movie theater. I was hoping for something a little deeper than that in a relationship."

"So, what, we're just gonna be fuck buddies?"

"Sure, friends that fuck. You go do who you wanna do, and if you ever need a friend, call me."

"Just like that? I take care of you all year and get you into the community and then as soon as recognition's over, you bolt?" Terry's sharp tone implied I owed her some huge favor. Terry's erratic driving implied I was getting under her skin.

"I never asked for you to switch my sponsor to Henry. I never asked to be allowed in the community. Hell, Terry, I didn't even know the community existed. Just take me back to school and drop me off."

Terry corrected her course back toward school and away from Henry's. "Are you gonna hang out with Roberts?" she asked after a few blocks of silence.

"Her name is Mandy, but whether or not I'm going to hang out with her isn't your concern."

"Lex, your world would turn into shit if anyone found out about the things you've done this past year. It'd be a shame if people found out you used me to make your fourth-class year easier."

I couldn't believe Terry would even think about turning in one of her own but knew she had the charm to pull it off without implicating herself. My heart jumped into my throat as the thought of getting kicked out of the academy for homosexuality raced through my mind. It wasn't the potential of an abrupt departure from the Zoo that concerned me, it was the permanent assignment of my parents knowing why.

If there was one positive trait I had gleaned from Kendra, it was to stand up for myself. I knew the academy was where I wanted to be, and I knew being gay was who I was. I didn't want to be stuck in a relationship that was held together by the threat of being turned in for being gay at the academy. Getting out of this "relationship" with Terry was worth the risk of her turning me in. I would have to take the gamble that she wouldn't go to the trouble to do that.

"Terry, that's a shitty thing to say."

Terry pulled into a scenic overlook parking lot and put the car in park. The majestic mountain range view filled up the windshield. "You think I won't do it?" She was talking to me as if she was still the upperclassman and I was merely the low-life SMACK. I couldn't tell if she really might follow through on her threat or was just reaching for something to pull me back to her. Either way, the thought of her pulling such a catty stunt fueled my anger toward her.

"Terry, you do what you need to do. If that involves you trying to get me kicked out of the academy, then I guess I'll have to deal with that. I guess I just thought I meant a little more to you."

Terry stretched her arm out and put her hand on my thigh. The shivers I normally got from her touch were gone. I was starting to question my own attraction to her. Had it been an attraction based on the lure of the illegal? Did I react to the attention of an attractive upperclassman who took an interest in me? Maybe her attraction to me was founded on the very same principles, pursuing that which she wasn't supposed to have and enjoying the awestruck SMACK looking up to her.

"Terry, don't." I took her hand in both of mine, caressing it like a mother would stroke her child who had just lost a pet.

Terry received my caresses as an invitation and leaned in for a kiss. I moved away and saw the hurt look on her face.

"Fine." She surrendered and reeled her hand back to the steering wheel. She jerked the car into reverse to start us back toward the academy. I put my hand on hers and pushed the car back into park.

"Terry, can we come to a more peaceful end to this?"

"I just can't believe you used me like this," Terry said.

"I wasn't using you, Terry. Maybe I got caught up in the attention of a hot woman who took good care of me, but I didn't hook up with you to make my life as a SMACK easier. If anything, it just made it harder because of the double life I had to lead."

Terry appreciated the "hot woman" comment, and she nodded her head in understanding at the double life we led. "Can we still hang out?" she asked.

"Of course. You and I share a history, and no one can ever take that away. But maybe we should keep the history in the past and find a way to make a new future as friends."

"Any chance I can get some lip treats from you once in a while?" Terry said with a wink.

"Lip treats?"

"Kisses. You are a good kisser, you know."

I smiled. "Sure. I'd like that." I liked where this conversation was going now. Hell, I'd sleep with Terry again, so long as I didn't have to sit through another dull date with her.

Terry put the car in reverse and got us out of the parking lot and en route to school.

She dropped me off at the stairwell, so I knew she was headed back off campus after I got out.

"See ya, friend." I got out of the car.

"Hey," she yelled out the open window, beckoning me back to her car. "You still think I'm a hot woman?"

I laughed at her shallow question but humored her with the truth. "Yeah, I do."

"Cool." Again, the clever reply from a skilled communicator. She zipped away, and I walked toward the stairwell, surprised that I felt no pain from leaving Terry.

CHAPTER 45

After a quick shower, I navigated the halls of the fifth floor until I found Mandy's room.

"Come in please, sir or ma—" Mandy was still adjusting to life as a recognized fourth-class cadet.

"Hey Lex, what are you doing here?"

"Looking for you. Where's your roommate?"

"She vaporized as soon as we got released. Why were you looking for me?"

"I wanted to know if you wanted to go out."

"Like on a date?" Mandy asked.

"Yeah, like on a date."

"Sure, what'd you have in mind?"

"I thought maybe we could catch a movie or something," I heard myself say, although not sure I wanted to sit through another movie. Then again, I hadn't seen the first movie I'd been to that day.

"Would you mind if we just went somewhere and talked? Is that too boring for you?"

I shook my head back and forth. "No, that's even better."

We changed into shorts, T-shirts, and hiking shoes and headed toward the hilly dirt trail that ran under the academy's electric power lines. We kept up with each other during the steep inclines and let our legs run away with our bodies on the descents. And in between the peaks and valleys, we held engaging conversations about where and how we had grown up, what made us come to the academy, and where we wanted to go when we graduated. My desire for Mandy grew as each detail of her life unfolded. Having survived my first fling with Terry, it was refreshing to be at the beginning of my first real relationship.

CHAPTER 46

"So, is Mandy gonna be at your retirement ceremony tomorrow?"

"Yup."

In fact, Mandy, who had outpaced me in promotions and was now a full colonel, was going to be the presiding officer at my ceremony. We had remained very close friends, having endured our first year at the Zoo together, dating for two years, and then staying on very solid terms for our final year at the Academy and then our follow-on Air Force careers.

She may not have been my first relationship with a woman, but ours was my most significant relationship with a woman.

"What about Terry?"

Now there was a blast from the past. "I haven't thought about her in decades."

"I wouldn't mind another three-way with her."

"Kendra, is everything always about sex with you?"

"Yup."

"Then you should definitely pursue a two-way with Terry. You're perfectly suited for each other."

I shook my head, still amazed I had discovered who I truly was in an environment that didn't accept that truth. I had survived in a profession that not only didn't welcome, but persecuted my kind.

The other shocker was that my friendship with Kendra had survived. But that seemed to be our modus operandi…her thinking she knew what's best for me, acting on that ill-advised thought, me getting pissed off at her, and her somehow weaving her way back into a friendship with me. And for whatever reason, it worked. It wasn't perfect. It wasn't smooth. It defied the odds and made sense only to the two of us.

And just like leaving the uniformed Air Force for the civilian-attired Air Force, it was comforting to have a known quantity. Kendra was my constant, who rode out (and sometimes caused) the rough patches. She catalyzed me finding my voice and gave me an outlet when there was no one else I could tell.